Beyond Blue Ice

A Novel By:

Stanley K. Smith

Bloomington, IN

Milton Keynes, UK

AuthorHouse™
1663 Liberty Drive, Suite 200
Bloomington, IN 47403
www.authorhouse.com
Phone: 1-800-839-8640

AuthorHouse™ UK Ltd.
500 Avebury Boulevard
Central Milton Keynes, MK9 2BE
www.authorhouse.co.uk
Phone: 08001974150

First published by AuthorHouse 4/25/2007

ISBN: 978-1-4343-1137-5 (sc)

Printed in the United States of America
Bloomington, Indiana

This book is printed on acid-free paper.

For Larry, *The Bearman,*
and Lori.

We all fall in love, and we fall into life
We look for the truth on the edge of a knife.

. . . .

Freedom is ever deceiving,
Never turning out to be what it seems.

"Nobody Knows"
Dickey Betts
(Recorded by The Allman Brothers Band)

Chapter 1

THE CRASH

Ab Bailey was inching along quietly when he first heard the plane. It wasn't that uncommon in southeast Alaska to hear a jet, and, for a while, he paid it no attention. It was probably headed for Tok or Anchorage. At the moment, he had plenty on his mind anyway. He was in the middle of a belly-crawling stalk and was dead set on the hundred-pound caribou that was forty yards ahead. He needed ten more yards, and then he would wait until she turned broadside, or nearly broadside. He could have done her with a rifle from 300 yards, but what kind of challenge would that be?

The waist-high buckbrush and red willows were dry in September. With so little wind, Ab rattled something with every yard he crawled closer to the little herd of caribou. He had learned that Caribou usually move all the time, but this small herd of cows and yearlings were mostly lying down now, happy with the patch of moss and lichens they had found along the banks of the Chisana River.

Ab had his bow in front of him now. He would move it forward two feet, then inch toward it, slithering, and move it forward again. He thought he was busted when the old lead cow popped her head up, boring a hole with both eyes into the willow bush he was lying behind. But he knew she couldn't smell him so he just lay there, staring back up into the mighty Wrangell Mountains, which looked like an impressionist painting for twenty miles. There were reds and golds mixed with browns, grays, and the white snow higher up into the mountains.

Ab was lucky to have the breeze right, so she couldn't smell him. He didn't want to shoot the lead cow anyway. He wanted the little cow, especially for the backstraps and hams. The old cow went back to feeding, and Ab inched forward three more yards with the next breeze. He eased up on his knees and threaded an arrow onto the bowstring. It came back smooth, and Ab hit his anchor as the little animal munched away on a hunk of moss, no idea that a man had invaded her world.

Ab had killed around 600 big game animals with a bow and arrow, but he could never shake the adrenaline rush. With enough experience, you could control it somewhat, but any attempted murder of a living thing brought on certain body reactions. It didn't even matter if it was a rabbit. As soon as you set out to kill it, your blood pressure went up, sweating started, and the old heart rate would go from 70 to 150, in a hurry.

Ab had the rush as much in check as it was going to get as he settled the thirty-yard sight pin into the spot on her chest he wanted to hit. Then he dumped the bowstring. He could see it, as if in slow motion: her head was turning as the noise reached her before the arrow. He saw the chewing stop, moss hanging out of either side of her mouth. Then there was the sound of struck meat, a sound like a bat hitting a side of beef. He saw the white fletching disappear into her chest and then the animal churning up ground headed toward the river. She only made it thirty yards. The rest of the herd exploded into the shallow waters of the Chisana and disappeared into the brush on the other side.

Ab stood up and stretched, sore from the long belly crawl. He walked over to the dying animal on the riverbank. It was then that he thought he heard the jet again, but he couldn't be sure because the river was so noisy. He looked down at the animal, not quite dead. Blood was bubbling out of her nose and mouth, her eyes rolling back in her head. She was drowning in her own blood, Ab knew, the product of a double pneumothorax caused by the razor sharp broadhead through both lungs.

Most people, Ab thought, had no concept of how arrows or bullets killed things. They had the lame idea that it was instantaneous from watching idiotic TV shows and movies where people were blasted off their feet by nine millimeters and .380's. It didn't happen that way, Ab knew. It took time, and it took a bleedout, enough for the blood pressure to drop off where the brain couldn't get oxygen, shutting down the system. Ab bent down and stroked the animal's neck as her head stretched back and forth and her legs made their final kicks. Then it was over.

Just then, Ab was sure he heard the jet again. It was lower now, coming from the north. When he had heard it a few moments ago, it sounded like it was coming from the southeast. Although it was getting dark fast, now he could see the plane, much too low. The landing gear was down and the plane was headed right back into the Wrangells, the mountains it had apparently just come through a few moments before. No landing strips up there pal, Ab thought. Besides, the jet looked too low to do anything other than crash into the Snag Creek drainage.

Ab knew the elevation on this part of the Chisana was only 3,000 feet. The jet didn't look to be more than 4,000 feet over his head. The Wrangells here were eight to ten thousand feet high. The front range of the Wrangells was called the Nutzotin Mountains, and the jet was headed straight for them. As it went over Ab's head, he saw something moving. It was the landing gear being retracted. This pilot had a jet headed straight into the mountains, losing altitude, and he was pulling up his landing gear. It was then that Ab Bailey knew he was about to see a spectacular crash, one with apparently suicidal tendencies. Why else would the pilot turn the plane into the mountains and retract the landing gear? Maybe some electrical system was out of whack and the plane was doing it on its own. Didn't matter now; that baby would be scrap metal in the Snag Creek drainage in about five seconds. "Hope you people made peace with your maker," Ab thought.

But the jet didn't crash into the drainage. Amazingly, it cleared it. It disappeared, but Ab could still hear it. Then it happened. Ab could hear the sound of sheet metal ripping up ice, sliding and grinding for probably ten seconds. The pilot had tried to put it down on the glacier, the one just above the Snag Creek drainage, lying slightly underneath the highest peaks. All Ab heard now was the silence. Dead damn quiet. Alaska back to normal. Why should she give a shit? This country had soaked up a lot of aircraft over the years. There would be no sirens, no fire trucks, no ambulances to follow.

Ab stood back up, stretched a bit, and took a long look around. The Chisana was rolling good now, the water cold as ice. But icy water was the least of Ab's problems now. The challenge of getting onto the glacier to try to rescue any survivors was the problem. He had climbed it more than once with the Bearman, his friend who guided hunting parties throughout the area, and he knew that it was dangerous as hell, even on a sunny day with a partner.

Ab looked up at the sky with the snow clouds rolling in fast. It would be coming down tomorrow, hard and white, making life a slippery mess for a man on a mountainside. But there was no sense worrying about it until then. He couldn't attempt it this evening in any event. He would have to pack and plan for this little escapade. For now, he needed to get the little caribou butchered, pack it out to his four wheeler, and head to his cabin.

Ab could have ignored the plane crash if he were a different kind of man, could have let it be someone else's problem. But that would have been the empty man's answer. And there were no other men out here anyway, empty or otherwise. So he would have to face the real danger of dying tomorrow. It would gnaw at him during this one night, but if he blew it off his inaction would gnaw at him forever. There was no argument in his mind where that was concerned.

Chapter 2

HOLLY

Holly Allen had a problem. She was drop dead gorgeous. She was well aware of it. That's why, in eighteen years of acting, she never really got the big parts. She knew she was a good actress; she had been told so by lots of directors. But her looks were a little too stunning. If she had just been born a little uglier, like maybe a Meryl Streep or a Bette Davis, she could have gone places. It really didn't matter now. Her glory days were over anyway. At thirty-eight, you couldn't run in the Hollywood babe actress pack anymore. That was okay. Holly was smart. She didn't party too much and, thanks to her dad, had invested her money well. He was an investment banker in San Bernadino, living with Holly's mom in the same house she grew up in. From age twenty-one when she hit it big, he had invested her money for her. They still laughed about his craziest gamble for her. At age twenty-two, she got a $50,000 bonus check from profits off a movie she had been in.

"I never heard of it, Dad, what's it called again?" she asked.

"Well, uh, it's a little company called Microsoft, and I got a hunch it might take off. Anyway, we got you over 50K working in bonds and conservative stuff. I thought we'd just take a little chance for you. You're gonna make a lot more money, so I think it's worth the risk."

"Well, you're the brains in the family, Dad. Whatever you think."

It was the most money she would ever make. About every two weeks for ten years her dad would call her, always excited as hell, talking about how many times it had split, or how much it had gone up. So money wasn't Holly Allen's problem; it was men. Always had been, always would be.

She flat out didn't understand them, and had finally decided she didn't even like them that much. Married three times, no kids, nothing to show for it. All bad investments. The third one was a doozy. Alec Stoneberg had wined and dined her like a madman. She got all caught up in it. It wasn't just men that were stupid, she knew. Women were just as bad. And she was one of them. Alec, a big shot director, had cast her for the lead in his last loser movie. Like an idiot, she went into it knowing what he was up to. The stupid movie bombed before it was ever released because he was more interested in getting into her twat that getting into the film. They got married right in the middle of shooting. And as soon as he had her, he wasn't interested anymore. Didn't matter, he was so lousy in bed it wasn't worth the trouble. Within three weeks of the wedding she was hearing the rumors. He was already banging her little co-star who was ten years younger. And then she found out about his coke habit and how far in debt he was. You just can't see that shit when you're all a-flitter and infatuated, all caught up in the moment.

It seemed so unfair for women. Here she was, thirty-eight and in her sexual prime, still good looking, and she hadn't had sex in almost a year now. By choice. But she craved it every night. She wasn't a pervert. It was her body, the old biological clock screaming at her through her hormones, "Get me laid and get me laid now." So she did what any sensible woman of the new millennium would do. She bought sex toys online. Of course it wasn't exactly the same because there was no warmth, no nurturing, no conversation. Not that she had gotten much of that from her three husbands. She had gotten a lot of farting and snoring. At least those toys stayed quiet when you unplugged them.

A man's relationship with a woman seemed a lot like an hourglass to Holly. The man was the top part, full of sand, and the woman was underneath, accepting the sand as he poured it through. And the woman needed that sand, and it felt good coming into her life, a beautiful relationship starting up. Men were so eager at first, so giving, so kind, and so attentive as they let every grain of love seep through. But just like the hourglass, the old meter was running, and just when you got comfortable with that steady stream of sand, it started slowing down. The attention went away, the conversations shortened, and even though you fought it, you knew what the outcome would be. Instead of leaving while there was still room for more sand, you just hung in there and denied the obvious. Then the last grain fell, the hour was up, and the man was gone. Evaporated, empty glass, with no more steady stream of love pouring in. Where was that man who never ran out of sand, Holly wondered. Had they just quit making them. They certainly used to be in good supply.

But Holly Allen knew she had no right to complain. On the surface, she was living the ultimate fantasy life. Born gorgeous in California, smack dab in the middle of the beautiful people, with a relatively successful acting career. Not one in one million little girls would ever grow up to live the life that Holly Allen was living. And good for them, she thought. Holly had finally decided that everyone famous in southern California was exactly the same. They were all perfect, and they were all worthless. Like the three beautiful wedding cakes she had. You start cutting into them and the "pretty" is all gone. Just sugar and fat and instant gratification. And tomorrow morning, you feel guilty for ever putting one goddamn bite in your mouth. The men that came with those cakes were no different. But then again, neither was Holly, she thought to herself.

Holly kept her chin up anyway. It was the life and the lifestyle she had, so she would go ahead and live it. Having three bad marriages was not good by any standard, but in this part of the world, it made her a lightweight. She had friends who had been married eight times, shaking off divorces and moving on as if they had lost a few ballgames over the course of the season, but still had a shot at the playoffs.

Marriage in Hollywood was more about jockeying for position than love anyway. People didn't get married for love out here, she thought. It was about prestige, and pomp and circumstance. Career advancement was high on the list too. Lifetime commitment—well, if it worked out that way, that was fine.

But you didn't think about things at thirty-eight the way you did at twenty-five. And Holly Allen's thinking was getting progressively worse. She still had that fabulous smile on the outside, but there was a gradually increasing frown on the inside. She had seen it in older actresses when she was young. The resentment toward the younger, prettier actresses was palpable. "They're getting my parts" was what they were thinking. Then the panic sets in, along with the bitterness, and suddenly an old girl's best friend is her plastic surgeon. Holly had made her mind up about that. She was not going that route, becoming a caricature of a younger, prettier woman with skin re-stretched so tight that the lips get wider by an inch and the eyes have an oriental slant. They looked passable on the screen, but up close, it was a scary thing. No ma'am, Holly thought. Just go away with a little grace and dignity, even if that meant without a good man by your side, or a child or two. She had never even come close to getting that.

That was the bitch of it all. She seemed to be just one generation from the people who made it work. Like her parents and most of their friends. They were really able to pull it off. That til death do you part crap. Whatever. She wasn't getting into any more of that philosophical, cultural shit on a Thursday night. She had a script to read tomorrow.

Chapter 3

AB

Ab retrieved his backpack and knelt down over the small caribou he had just killed. He felt a bit more pressed for time now, caused by the nervous energy that attends the anticipation of what you dread to come. Ab began fishing in his backpack for his scalpel bag, which was a Crown Royal bag holding two handles and a box of blades. Just as he found it, he caught movement down the riverbank. It was a bear. A very big bear at that, an eight-foot silvertip grizzly trundling down the Chisana shoreline on the fall feedup.

Bumping into bears was a common thing in this part of the world. Ab had been coming up here so many years now that seeing large numbers of animals every day was commonplace. He had learned a lot about their nature and how to relate to them. Ab saw the bear about the same time it came around a big rock and saw him. They were sixty yards apart. Ab stood up slowly, and the bear, as if it were mocking him, stood up on his hind legs. It was nothing to get too worked up about, but Ab was standing over a freshly killed caribou. The big bear started working his nose. He knew that bears ate everything they could this time of year, and would be sound asleep deep in a den in about six weeks.

The bear had the scent of blood now and probably wasn't going away. At least not without a little coaxing. From a crossdraw holster Ab eased out a big single action Ruger .480 and put the sights just below and two feet left of the bear. He knew exactly how these big boys operated. Bearman always said, "They're ruthless bastards. They'll get away with what they think they can without getting hurt. Show 'em you can hurt 'em, they'll go away."

Ab wasn't really crazy about his .480. It was heavy for a handgun and louder than holy hell. The recoil was pretty stiff too, as it launched a 400 grain bullet at 1300 feet per second, all of which made it the perfect handgun for bad bear country. He thumb-cocked the hammer while the big griz swung his head from side to side, sizing up his chances for supper. From this point on it was all sights and trigger control. The boom was gigantic, echoing down the river. The 400 grainer went right where he wanted it, kicking up a spray of rocks from the gravel bar. The bear's legs and neck were peppered. He beat a quick path into the willows and was gone.

With that little problem solved, Ab took a Number 22 scalpel blade, attached it to a handle and made quick work of the caribou, constantly looking over his shoulder. He slid the hams and the backstraps in a black garbage bag and into his backpack. Normally, Ab would not leave any meat behind, but he had other matters on his mind this evening. Besides, it was already 10 p.m., with no daylight left, a one-hour walk to the four wheeler, and a big griz out there in the alders with a fix on things, so he decided to be prudent and bug out. Old Ephraim deserved a good meal anyway. He grabbed his bow and started south, going upriver toward his four wheeler, thinking about the plane and the people on board.

Ab had been raised in Alabama, mostly by his father's little brother, Yulner Devon Bailey. He vaguely remembered the fight over custody because he was so young at the time. Ab's father, Yul D's older brother, was a Birmingham attorney. His mother was a nurse. On the way home from the Shelby County Bar Christmas Party in 1976, they were broadsided by a drunk. His father was killed instantly, and his mother lived for three days. Ab was seven at the time. Guardianship was awarded to his mother's oldest sister, Ab's Aunt Agnes. If she couldn't serve, the honor went to Yul D, although Ab was told in later years that that was a point of much contention between his parents when drafting the Will. Yul D was six foot three, 225 pounds of tough. A retired marine colonel, he had more Vietnam stories than Agnes had figurines.

What Ab did remember was Aunt Agnes's little house in Mountain Brook, the one that put Ab into the correct school system. He hated it from the git-go. He didn't like the snooty little rich kids, and he most assuredly didn't like the rigidity of stuffy old Aunt Agnes. He wanted to live on the farm with Yul D. He told Yul D as much when he called Lowndes County and talked to him three nights a week. Ab couldn't exactly remember it now, but he knew it was Yul D who put the ideas in his little skull. With enough truancy, fighting, and downright meanness at home, old Agnes might just give it up and ship his young ass off for some military style discipline. It took almost a year, but by the Fall of 1977, she threw in the towel, called Yul D and told him to come get him. Ab remembered her exact words on the phone. From down the hall he could hear her. "Yulner, I suspect you're partly behind this. At worse, you probably put this negativism in his head, and at best, you are a member of the odious Bailey gene pool with which I wish my sister had never become involved. The boy is uncontrollable. Due to his paternal pedigree, I doubt there is much that can be salvaged. Come and get him." At the time, Ab thought that a paternal pedigree must be an odor. He had, after all, refused to bathe for several weeks, pitching total tantrums on the subject. Good. He'd take a bath on the farm in Lowndes County.

That was thirty years, a bad marriage, and lots of rounds down range ago. He had his ups and downs with Yul D over the years too. Yul D was 28 when he picked up Ab. He had a 7,200-acre spread willed to him and Ab's father by Grandpa Bailey. So technically, half of it was Ab's. Yul D ran a firearms academy and hunting club on the property, so Ab just grew up immersed in that culture. Yul D's second wife Ina always referred to all the gun nonsense as arcane minutiae. "The very idea," she said, "of grown men sitting around for hours discussing the proper angle for a secondary cut on a sear in a 1911." It was stuff you didn't learn in school, especially not in Mountain Brook, Alabama. Ab considered himself God-given lucky. He knew the correct angle for a secondary cut on a sear in a 1911.

As Ab finished with the caribou, he contemplated his trip up to the glacier the next day. He had the mental toughness that had been hammered into him by Yul D and the rudimentary climbing skills he had learned from the Bearman. But the bottom line was that it might take more mental skill and muscle mass than he had.

Chapter 4

BLUE ICE

Ab shouldered his pack and washed the caribou blood from his hands in the Chisana. He didn't really mind the two-mile hike south to his four wheeler. It was easy even in the dark—all upstream alongside the roaring Chisana River. The noise kept a man's mind fresh and clean, and moving hard always made it easier to think. But he couldn't help wondering why a small jet would be in this part of the world this late in the day. It made no sense to him, and in all likelihood he would never have an answer.

Out of habit, Ab would glance over his shoulder every few minutes as he walked along. He was, after all, carrying forty pounds of fresh caribou meat on his back. With the river noise, it would be easy to get snuck up on. It was another lesson he had learned young from Yul

D: check your six and check it often. Even covered in the scent of caribou meat, however, Ab knew it would be unlikely that a bear would attack him. It wasn't their M.O. They usually took the proactive approach, sizing up an opponent by stomping and woofing and cracking limbs. They wanted to sound dominant. That's why you never made eye contact with a bear. It was a challenge, and they might just take you up on it.

Thank heavens there weren't very many big cats this far north because they were a different story. If a cougar was on his trail, he would probably never know it until the takedown. Ab had heard stories of sightings from the old trappers, but he had yet to see one in twelve seasons of stomping around this country. He thought about an article he once read about the Indian Sundarban, where the fishermen wore masks on the backs of their heads to avoid man-eating tigers. If there were tigers up here, Ab thought, he would have just walked out backwards.

With a half-mile walk left, Ab could make out the Snag Creek drainage ahead. He could see the skyline above it where the beautiful Nutzotin Mountains backed into the Wrangells. They weren't as high as the Coast range with only a few topping ten thousand feet, but Ab always thought they had honor and dignity. Of course, now they had the remains of a plane crash too. This time, he simply couldn't take in the beauty of the scene because he would have to climb it tomorrow, and what was beautiful from this distance would be treacherous up close.

Ab found the Honda and unshouldered his load. He stretched his back out, contemplating tomorrow morning's route up to the crash site. It wouldn't be the first time, of course. Bearman had made sure of that a couple of years back.

Bearman loved glacier ice. He called it blue ice. "Wildman, it's pure, uncivilized, unfilthitized, blue ice," he had said. He always called Ab the Wildman. During his third season of trapping and guiding around the Chisana with Bearman, they had had a group of sheep hunters cancel in late August so they had ten days to scout and goof off. Bearman was studying the mountains one morning after breakfast when he turned to Ab and said, "Hey, Wildman, I got a good idea. You know that fine brown whiskey you been lugging up here every year. "

"You wanna start drinking Jack Daniels at ten a.m.?"

"No. But I'd like some blue ice in my drink this evening. And the way I figure it, it'll just about be the cocktail hour when we get back from the top of that glacier."

The idea was ludicrous, in Ab's mind. But he knew the Bearman, and once he had an idea—even a stupid one—he wouldn't let it go. He also knew that Bearman could pull it off. He had the moxie and brains to get it done. Bearman had an I.Q. at least as high as his own, which had been tested to be 138. Ab had a B.A. and a law degree, while Bearman had quit school in the ninth grade. Didn't matter. They were two men living the way they wanted to. They were renegades in a part of the world where you were supposed to be.

Ab knew good and well that blue ice wasn't the sole reason that Bearman wanted to climb up to that glacier. Bearman had dead time on his hands, and he wanted a challenge. Although he loved blue ice in his whiskey because of the intense flavor it added, the climb itself was the end game for him. Ab didn't want to do it. It made no sense to him to climb 4,500 vertical feet just to hear some blue ice clinking around in his whiskey glass, but, then again, arguing with the bull-headed Bearman all day could be worse than the fear of falling four thousand feet. And, once challenged, Ab Bailey wasn't likely to back down.

Standing by his four wheeler now, looking up into the mountains with snow clouds rolling in, Ab dreaded the thought of climbing that glacier the next day alone. Climbing up with a partner to get blue ice on a sunny day might be one thing, but alone in a blowing snow with the possibility of finding badly injured people took any possible pleasure of this hike right out of Ab's mind. He hoped he could make it to the crash site. He was a tough, determined man, without a doubt, but he was no Bearman.

It was so easy for the Bearman. He was raised in this country; and he knew it perfectly. His dad, who came to this country in the fifties, was the first white outfitter in the Wrangells. Hunters came into camp the same way they did now, on Beavers and Otters and Super Cubs on floats. From there, it was on trains of horses loaded with panniers. They had small cabins as base camps on the various lakes dotted across the Chisana River valley. From there, it was mostly backpack or horseback to the various spike camps.

Henry Kampet had four sons. Henry Kampet Outfitting became Kampet and Sons Outfitting in 1965 when his second son was born. Jordy Ray was the fourth and last Kampet boy, and he was the toughest. He was the only son who had stayed with the business, and for all practical purposes it was his now. He was in charge of every aspect of the operation, but bear hunting was his forte, which had earned him his nickname.

Bearman looked the part. He was six foot two, 180 pounds of rawboned man. He looked strong, and was stronger than he looked. His hair was long, curly, and dirty blond like a lion's mane. He kept it long, probably for the same reason Ab did, to piss off the old man, or Yul D, or any other oppressive motherfucker for that matter. Bearman had blue eyes and Slavic features with a small nose.

Ab liked to kid himself and think he was the second toughest person in southeast Alaska, but he wasn't. That would be Lauren Kampet, the Bearman's wife, a five foot four inch 110 pound Canadian woman of Scandinavian descent. Quiet and self-effacing, she could run a back-hoe, a D6, a chainsaw, or portable sawmill, and she could wrangle horses better than any man Ab ever met, save the Bearman himself.

Bearman and Lauren got along well, but not because of Bearman. He was as stubborn and strong-willed as hell itself, while Lauren was easy going, which made for a good fit. Still, they argued frequently, in the way of frontier couples. Amazingly, Bearman lost a lot of arguments, which was good, because if Lauren really put her foot down, Bearman was usually wrong. Then he would get pissed and rant at Ab.

"Goddamn Scanderhoovian stiff-willed old bag," he'd say. "I'll tell you Wildman, I do not understand women." Then he'd shake his big blond mane. "It's a shame that that beautiful plumbing comes with such fucked up wiring."

Bearman's stubbornness was a strong thing. His ability to will himself through a problem was what Ab would need for tomorrow, but with the kind of weather he would be facing, all the willpower and skill he possessed might not be enough. He could have had an army of Bearmen with him and still dreaded going up on that glacier in search of the crash site because, in the end, each man would have to climb under his own power as he struggled to make that ascent. But Ab didn't even have the one Bearman with him now. He tried to get it in his head. He tried to remember the first time up, with all the pitfalls and the scary parts, Bearman laughing at him the whole time. Unlike this time where he had no choice, the first time he was just plain goaded into it by Bearman.

As Ab bungied his pack on the back of his Honda, he noticed that he could not make out the mountains now. The clouds had taken away the contrast of land and sky. He cranked the four wheeler and started down the winter trail. It was a long muddy trail back to the cabin. Ab was driving on auto-pilot, just following his muddy tracks from earlier in the day. He stopped at the Snag Creek crossing on the trail. He would head the four wheeler as high up the drainage as he could get it tomorrow—just as he and Bearman had done on the first climb, several years back.

Ab remembered the original climb, and he knew that he was in just as good condition as he was then. Although he was only five foot ten and weighed only 160 pounds, Ab was, at age thirty-seven, in tremendous shape. He was not a big-boned man. He had slim hips, broad shoulders, and not much body fat. He talked fast, moved fast, and thought fast. Truth was, he could outwalk the Bearman, but climbing up vertical walls just didn't appeal to him. Ab remembered back to the first climb.

They had taken the Honda 450 for six miles and then up the drainage until it got too steep. From there, it was two and one half miles of class three scrambling, and west down a narrow ledge for about 300 yards, with a drop off of 500 vertical feet. That spooked Ab, but not the Bearman. He just walked down the two-foot ledge like he didn't have a concern in the world, while Ab inched along hugging the rocks. Bearman had to stop and wait on Ab twice. The second time he tucked his thumbs under his armpits and started bobbing his head and making chicken noises.

"Fuck you, you son of a bitch," Ab had said, but couldn't help laughing as he watched his friend chicken dance on a two-foot ledge in the middle of Alaska.

The next part was nothing to laugh at. It was a true eighty-foot vertical climb, with just a few hand and foot holds. It was that part of the original climb that Ab mostly remembered this evening. Doing it tomorrow, in the snow, would take all his nerve, and all his minor league climbing skills. It would have been a piece of cake for an experienced climber, which Ab was not.

Bearman had stopped Ab at the base on the first climb. "You wait here off to the side til I get on top and give you the go ahead. That way, if I pull a peeler, you won't go down with me."

"Why don't you wait here, directly beneath me," Ab had said, "because I know I'm gonna pull a peeler and when I do, I want your ass going all the way to the bottom with me."

"Easy now," Bearman had said. "This is gonna be a piece of cake, you just watch how it's done." With that, he grabbed a hunk of rock, got his foot on a good spot, and started up. Ab watched for a minute or two, but started getting dizzy from looking up, so he just hugged the rocks and waited for the death cry. In about ten minutes he heard Bearman yell down from the top. "Wait just one minute, Wildman."

"How about I just wait 'til you get your damn blue ice and come on down."

"Nope, we got to fill up both packs." And with that, Ab heard something flopping down the rocks. A climbing rope slid by him and the end stopped fifteen feet lower.

"I brought a hundred-foot rope in case there were any pussies on this trip," Bearman said.

"Well, ain't you clairvoyant, because there is a pussy on this trip, and he don't mind cheating his way to the top." The Bearman had laughed and screamed something or other about all the beautiful blue ice he was standing on. Ab didn't pay much attention to him as he was too focused on securing the rope and making the climb up. He wasn't comfortable even when he was tied off.

That was the key to this country, Ab knew. It wasn't just outdoor skills; it was knowing what equipment you needed and having it when you needed it. Ab knew he couldn't just take off from camp half-assed to go find a crashed plane. This was unforgiving land, and without the right clothing and equipment you either toughed it out or you died. Ab remembered a quote from Ray Jardine, a man who backpacked the entire Pacific Crest Trail with a twelve-pound pack. When asked how he got by with so little, he replied, "If I need it and I don't have it, then I don't need it."

Bearman's strength was that he never took off through the Alaskan bush without seriously considering what he needed. And that included bringing what other people needed, even if they didn't. So it didn't totally surprise Ab when he saw the rope sliding by him on the first climb up to the glacier.

Ab had pulled himself over the top that day, onto the blue ice of the glacier. They ate a casual lunch while admiring the view. It was cool on the ice, but probably not below fifty degrees. August in Alaska saw warm days when the sun was shining. Bearman had started in on a slab of the ice after lunch, chipping away to beat hell. After filling both packs, he laid back on the ice and surveyed his territory.

"Look at the damn view, Wildman. We are a coupla lucky bastards. Can you imagine living in a city elbow to elbow with all those turd-sucking flatlanders. Now wouldn't that suck?"

"I've done it," Ab said. "And some days it does suck."

Bearman had gotten up and peered down from the glacier, looking into the drainage. "We need to get a move on, Wildman." With that, he fished two carabiners out of his pack and handed one to Ab.

"Shouldn't be that bad going down," Ab said. "An easy rappel to the ledge, and then the death march over to the drainage."

Bearman rappelled down the rope first and called back up to Ab. Ab slid off the ice and ran the rope through his shoulder straps and onto the carabiner. He had made it safely to the narrow ledge without incident. Bearman looked back up at the rope. "I guess it'll be there til we get back next week."

"Fuck that noise," Ab had said.

Ab would definitely need that rope. Tomorrow. In the snow and the wind. And no climbing partner to get up that damn vertical wall. "Just stay in the moment, Ab. Get back to the cabin. Get a good night's sleep," he thought. He would worry about it when the time came.

Chapter 5

THE RUSE

Holly hadn't totally given up. While she suspected that there weren't any real men left in southern California, that didn't mean there might not be one somewhere else in the world. In fact, she had now had two dates with a foreign gentleman by the name of Matra Langdor. Matra apparently lived on, and owned, a large portion of Sri Lanka. He had explained it all on their first date when he had rented an entire restaurant for the evening. All Holly knew about Sri Lanka was that it was a tear-drop shaped island off the coast of India, that it used to be called Ceylon, and that she had no intention of ever going anywhere near the place. But it was amusing to spend some time with someone from another culture to see how the other half lives.

Holly met Matra at one of those posh Hollywood parties where the women watch the women, and the men walk around with that cocky demeanor that says, “Hey, I don’t know shit about being a real man, but don’t I look cool.” It applied to her, as well. Outside of acting like someone else, she didn’t know anything about the real world either. In her part of the world everybody got everything they wanted all the time. No one at that party had the foggiest idea how to build, fix, grow, or make anything. Just like the movies they made, it was all a fucking hoax. Yet they made all the money.

Matra, on the surface at least, seemed to be a breath of fresh air. He was polite to a fault, and he had homed in on Holly the second she walked into the room. She had actually gotten a call telling her that a secret admirer would be there. She got those calls a lot, so she didn’t think much of it at the time.

Holly Allen was a short woman for an actress. Five foot three, brunette. Her lack of height had held her back from getting some very good parts in the past. At parties like this, she avoided the buffet areas like the plague. Pure willpower had kept her at 105 pounds for 20 years now. Matra seemed to want to hover over the food. He was strikingly larger than Holly—around six foot two, 225, she guessed, and a little soft looking. But he had very nice features. Holly had no intention of ever having sex with him, not from the start, and she wasn’t going to lead him on about it either. But he was not pushy. On both dates, he had done no more than kiss her on the cheek.

On their first date where he had booked the entire restaurant, Holly got the guided tour of Matra's life. It was indeed one of privilege. His grandfather was English, the rest of his ancestors Indian. He was not so dark as a full-blooded Indian, though his hair was black and graying slightly. His eyes were greenish brown, and that's what caught your attention most about his appearance. His grandfather, as a Lord of the British commonwealth, had acquired a large estate in the '40's, and it was still in the family. It was totally his now, being the only son of an only son. Women didn't inherit in that part of the world. Another reason never to set foot in the place, Holly thought.

The family estate was divided into the production of tea, rubber, rice and coconuts. The total estate was over 200,000 hectares, or 800,000 acres. There was no Mrs. Langdor. Holly had figured that part out already.

On the second date, he had finally gotten to it. Perhaps she would like to come visit his estate sometime. So that was it; he was wife shopping. The clincher for Holly was when he told her that his wife had died giving birth to their seventh child two years ago. What to weigh, what to weigh. On the one hand, she could go to this third-world luxury estate and be a baby factory and trophy wife for this guy, or she could just hang out here with the Hollywood dickheads. It was an easy choice.

Matra would never approve of her toys anyway. He was too old fashioned.

She tried to tell him, in a polite way, and could see the disappointment on his face.

"Oh, well," he said. "I have to fly to San Francisco for one last contract negotiation, and after that, as soon as the jet is ready, I am flying home."

She couldn't help but ask him how he knew about her. How did a man from Sri Lanka know that Holly Allen existed. His disappointment went away for a moment and he laughed.

"You don't know? Most Sri Lankan men think you are the most beautiful woman alive. Your movies are shown constantly there."

"I'll be damned," Holly thought. She needed to look into this; she might be missing some royalties. With the mood lighter, Matra asked her to fly to San Francisco with him for a farewell date. Holly didn't want to, and she knew the entire evening would be a hard sales package by this guy, but he had been a perfect gentleman to her, so she agreed. She did make it clear right then that it would be their last date.

Chapter 6

MATRA

If the Allen woman wouldn't come to Sri Lanka voluntarily, Matra Langdor would kidnap her. It was that simple. His man in charge of security on the island, Rusty, would plan it out. He was an American, after all, and ex-American military. Holly Allen was beautiful, and Matra could understand why her movies were so popular in Sri Lanka. But he didn't need her for love; he needed her on his arm to win the next presidential election. He might be able to pull it off without her, he knew, but with her as his wife, it was a guarantee.

Matra and his entourage had been in L.A. for three weeks, ostensibly on a business trip. The entire trip to America, however, was for the sole purpose of getting Holly Allen back to Sri Lanka. It had looked promising to Matra at first, and he thought he might be able to pull it off without resorting to criminal activity. But he knew as soon as their first date was over that she would not go with him. At least not voluntarily. These idiotic American women. How had they come to be so independent. It was the fault of the American men, no doubt. They had lost control somewhere along the line. Matra knew how to take control of a woman. You do it by force.

Rusty had come up with the plan. "Just get her on the plane," he had said. Once in the air on a private jet he would take control of the situation and get her in line. "She can play the wife, or she can play the widow, her choice," he said. Matra Langdor knew that Rusty was the perfect man for the job. He was intimidating, and he could be the definition of brutality. In fact, Matra knew that the hardest part of the operation would not be scaring the woman into line; it would be keeping Rusty from killing her if she resisted. Of course, it was exactly what would have to be done. But it would have to be done delicately, without any odor of suspicion hanging over the death. That would probably be the end result anyway, he knew. At some point, she would have to go. Just get through the election, Matra thought. The rest of it could be handled by Rusty. When it came to killing and all its various methods and nuances, Rusty was without peer.

So the plan was laid. Rusty had worked out the details.

"You got to get her on the plane voluntarily, Mr. Langdor. People have to see her get on your plane without being forced. I'll take it from there. For the trip over, I think it would be best if you were not on the plane. Just me and the boys. I'll indoctrinate her on the way. Trust me, by the time we get to Colombo, she'll be so scared she won't dare screw up. Besides, she's an actress; she knows how to play parts. And her payment for this role will be that she gets to live, for awhile."

"What about her personal things, her passport, luggage. She won't get on a plane with any of that just to fly off for a dinner date," Matra said.

"I've thought about that, sir. We'll get a team into her apartment when she leaves for the airport. They can get her things. Then we'll fly the long way around. I talked to your pilot. We'll swing up north with the woman over Canada and southeast Alaska, stop over for fuel in Seoul, then on down to the island. You can go ahead, and we'll fly her personal items commercial to arrive ahead of us. It's all planned. The key part is up to you. Talk her into a dinner date. Promise her the moon. Whatever. She just has to get on board voluntarily. Once we are in the air, I'll handle it. It'll work. I guarantee it, sir."

At the time, Matra told Rusty he didn't think he could talk her into it.

"Sure you can, sir. Catch her during one of her weak moments. She's a woman. She'll have plenty of those."

Typical American army man, Matra thought. Always overconfident.

Rusty intimidated Matra despite the fact that Matra was his boss. But he knew his operation would not work without a man as brutal as Rusty at the security helm. Rusty had been with him for several years now. He knew the man had fought in the Gulf war and that he had obviously had some legal problems in the States years before. But whatever his problems had been, he kept them tucked inside and did his job with brutal efficiency. The man appeared to have no conscience when it came to disposing of an enemy. Matra knew that no matter what the Middle Eastern world thought about the lack of resolve of America, if the country kept turning out soldiers like Rusty, there would always be hell to pay in the end for provoking those people.

So Matra did what Rusty said. He caught the woman in a light moment and talked her into a dinner date in San Francisco. Get her on the jet voluntarily. That's all he had to do. Then, by next year, he would be running the entire country of Sri Lanka. The island would be his. He would very likely be a widower again shortly thereafter. That should help his popularity. Sympathy for a man's personal tragedies was always a good thing.

Chapter 7

THE DATE

Holly slept late Friday morning. Then she went through a script for a made-for-TV movie her agent had sent her. It was total shit. Predictable lines, gaudy outfits, and, after the first scene, she finds out her darling husband has two other wives. To add insult to injury, the two other wives were being played by much younger actresses. So Holly was playing the old first wife, the bag who was really getting drug through it. They'd probably air it on the Women's Channel or Lifetime Network about thirty minutes after the director yelled "that's a wrap." Holly loved the Women's Channel because not only were all men pigs, but a goodly number of them were murderers too. And they always got what was coming to them at the end of the show, unlike real life. But this script was pretty lame, and she didn't need to do it unless she just wanted to. But if she did, it would probably go over like gangbusters in Sri Lanka.

Around four, she finally showered and got ready for her date with Matra. Just have a nice dinner and be nice to the guy, she thought. Besides, flying on a private jet was always fun. She was careful with her wardrobe this evening. She knew good and well she was still a knockout, so there was no reason to get this guy's hormones raging. He'd start up with the invitations again. She put on a beige skirt, white blouse and black pumps. The skirt had a matching jacket, all of it wool. She always got cold on airplanes and it was always damp and chilly in San Francisco to her. She still looked stunning. Couldn't help it.

Just like Matra said, the limo showed up at exactly 6:30. He was going to meet her at the plane. It took about forty-five minutes to get from Holly's house to the Longbeach Airport. Holly was escorted through the terminal quickly, only being recognized once, so she only signed one autograph. The people under twenty-five almost never knew who she was. "Getting old and unfamous, sweetheart," she said to herself.

Two young Indian-looking men escorted her out across the tarmac, where she felt hot in her wool suit.

"Where's Matra?" Holly asked one of the young men.

"Meester Langdor has been delayed for a few minutes due to beezness. He will be here soon. Pleeze board the plane and have a cocktail." She was no more than in a swiveling captain's chair before one of the men brought her a glass of red wine.

"I'll take chardonnay, if you have it," she said.

He put his arms out and raised his palms upward. "This is what we have," he said.

Oh hell, she thought, just drink it, relax, and get the damn date over with. She was still hot from the walk, and this jet, like every other one she had gotten on, didn't seem to have working AC until it was in the air.

Before Holly even finished the first glass of wine she wasn't feeling exactly right. Getting drunk too fast for one glass. She leaned over toward the young man standing nearby. "Excuse me," she said, "could you see if you can get some air going in here. I'm feeling a little faint."

He just smiled and continued to stare at her. He was probably in shock. Being that close to the Queen of Sri Lanka and all. Now she couldn't get her thoughts to mesh. She was getting seriously dizzy. She was going to pass out. From only one damn glass of wine. She was going fast. Her eyes were closed now. She could hear and feel a door being shut. She felt like she was in a vault. But the vault was starting to move. And then she passed out.

Chapter 8

THE TAO OF AB

Ab Bailey rode along on his four wheeler, thinking about tomorrow's problems and wondering if anyone could have possibly survived the crash. After crossing Snag Creek, he had eight or nine miles to the cabin. The cabin sat on a steppe above Carden Lake. In the daylight, you could see the entire Nutzotin mountain chain and the glaciers that fed the various streams and rivers coming down.

Ab tried to figure out what his options were as he drove the last few miles. Other than making the climb up alone, he could get up in the morning and drive to Jahtamund Lake where the Bearman and Lauren were. But that would mean a two day round trip, at best. Anyone who survived that plane crash and needed medical attention could easily be dead before then. Besides, it would only add one more man to the climb. It wasn't worth the delay. Bearman had two moose hunters in his camp, but they weren't in good enough shape to be of any help.

Ab rolled up to his cabin just before midnight. He stowed the caribou in the meat shed and then went inside and cranked up the woodstove to knock the chill and dampness out of the cabin. He poured himself a shot of Jack Daniels and ate a cold supper.

He was thinking a lot about planes this evening. He had flown on just about every kind of plane there was. He didn't like any of them. He didn't like to be on them. But he hated jets the most. Hearing one crash on a glacier didn't help his opinion of them any. If these people had been on a Beaver or Twin Otter, on floats, they could have swung down and landed right on his lake. It was two miles long. But not on a jet. On a bush plane you could fly second seat and talk to the pilot to see if anything was wrong. And if the goddamned propellers quit turning, you would know it.

On a commercial jet airliner, you were just a slave. You were trading freedom for time saving. You could only have a weapon on a jet if you snuck it on, which meant only bad guys had weapons on commercial jets. Ab couldn't help wondering what would have happened on 9/11 if those planes had had a few good men carrying concealed weapons. So he just traveled by truck. It took longer to go places, but he was pretty sure there had never been a terrorist in his Toyota, and it was slap full of guns.

Could those people on that jet have survived, he wondered. If he didn't die climbing up there tomorrow, he'd find out. Dying in a plane crash had to be worse than dying in a car wreck. He heard about it on TV all the time. If you died in a car crash, you only lost your life. If you died in a plane crash or ship wreck, you were a lost "soul." Losing your life would be bad enough, but losing your soul—that sounded pretty final.

Ab took a whore bath after cleaning his dishes and then wiped down the .480 with rem-oil. He stretched out on a lower bunk and started to read a few chapters from the *Tao Te Ching*. He had the entire text almost memorized, and it always amazed Bearman that Ab would want to read the same goofy Chinese book over and over again. Ab's little copy was totally careworn, as it was constantly being thrown into a pack or a duffle or stuffed into a pocket. This evening he picked up on Chapter 48.

In the pursuit of learning, everyday something is acquired.
In the pursuit of the Tao, everyday something is dropped.
Less and less is done, until non-action is achieved.
When nothing is done, nothing is left undone.

The world is ruled by letting things take their course.
It cannot be ruled by interfering.

What Ab took from the verse was that he didn't need anything. He was a whole individual. He didn't need anything that wasn't already there. Provided by nature, if you will. The problem, as Ab saw it, was to accept that freely and completely. The problem was to get rid of the accretions, the baggage that piled up in a man over the years. When those were gone, you could become fully human again. Easier said than done. It was funny, Ab thought. He watched bears and moose and deer going about their business often while in the bush. They had no problem with it. A deer never had a problem being a deer, or a bear a bear. But humans, we had a big problem. Most bespectacled old shrinks would tell us we needed to learn more about ourselves. We needed more money, a bigger house, faster car. And lots of pills to ease the reality of it all.

Lao Tsu got it right all those years ago in the backwoods of China: let go of the junk. You don't need more; you need less. Anytime Ab got nervous or insecure like he was this evening, he would try to think about that. It was all already there. Everything he needed, right inside his own skin. It was the other stuff, the shit he let get inside him, that was the problem. So thinking about tomorrow, this evening, was not the answer. Get up early, pack properly, and go do the job. That was all there was to it. Forget about the spooky shit until it occurred. Just deal with it when it happens, not before.

So Ab tried to quit interfering with tomorrow, but he couldn't quit wondering if he fell off that cliff and died, would he lose his life, or would it be his soul. He drifted off to sleep.

Chapter 9

NORTH TO ALASKA

Holly Allen was having a dream. In it, she was on a fast train. It was smooth and floaty, like one of those trains that rode on a magnetized rail in Japan. What was she doing in Japan? Then her eyes opened. There were four men sitting around her, and they weren't Japanese. And then she remembered. The plane was headed to San Francisco. She rubbed her eyes and pushed her hair back behind her ears. She realized she had one shoe on and one shoe off. Her head was hurting like hell.

"When do we get to San Francisco?"

Not one of the men said a word.

She rubbed her temples and looked around the plane. "Where's Matra?"

Still no answer. She looked around again. "Where the hell is Matra and where the hell am I?"

One of the younger men got up and walked to the cockpit. After a minute, a new man came back. He was older, a white guy, and pretty tough looking. She hadn't seen him before. He had a crew cut, a lot of muscles, and a pug nose that looked like an old golf ball. He leaned over her swivel chair, putting his big arms on the armrests.

"You'll be fine Miss Allen, just relax."

He said it nice, but he was obviously trying to be intimidating. It didn't work. He just reminded her of an old stunt guy, maybe a double for Charles Bronson or Sylvester Stallone.

"Get out of my damn face." She said it with authority, like she could back it up. Yeah, right. She was gonna get out of that chair and whip five guys' asses on a jet airplane. With what, a black pump?

He did back off. "I think we need to have a little talk, ma'am."

"So do I, and you can start by telling me where Matra is and where this fucking jet is going."

"Well, Mr. Langdor has gone ahead to Sri Lanka and would very much like for you to join him on his estate there. In fact, he left this morning."

"I told him, and I'm telling you, I am not going to Sri Lanka. Not now; not ever."

"I'm afraid that's a negative, ma'am. We're going there now."

She came up out of her seat and tried to hit him in the face. He caught her hand and tossed her back down like he would throw a housecat.

"Fuck you." Furious, just goddamn furious. "You're kidnapping me, that's what you're doing."

"We prefer to think of it more as a forced invitation."

"Who are you, what's your name?"

"My name is not important, but you can call me Rusty. I work for Mr. Langdor. I'm in charge of security at his estate. As you may or may not know, we've had quite a few problems with civil insurrections on the island in the past few years."

"Yeah, I get it. I'll bet that's your specialty, putting down insurrections and kidnapping women."

"My job is to do what Mr. Langdor asks of me, and for today that job is transporting you to his estate. We should arrive sometime mid-day tomorrow. Why don't you just make yourself comfortable and let Amran bring you a drink."

"I've already had one of his drinks."

"Yes, but this one will be clean, I guarantee it," Rusty said. She didn't need a drink. She needed to calm down and think. How would she get out of this mess. Her head was hurting so bad she couldn't put it all together. Screaming and yelling would do no good. It wasn't like she could storm a cockpit and fly a jet airplane back home. She just had to sit back and work out a plan.

Holly needed to know if there were any stops. What was the route? If she could get her hands on a phone, what would she tell someone. I'm on a plane, hijacked, and I have no idea where I'm at, but we're headed to Sri Lanka. What a goat fuck.

This morning she was sitting on her own couch reading a crappy TV manuscript, and twelve hours later she's kidnapped and on her way to the third world. Now there's a script for you. Nobody in Hollywood could dream this shit up. And the audacity of that bastard. She'd try to stay cool now, but if she ever got her hands on Matra Langdor, she would rip his goddamned lungs out with her fake fingernails. At least the guys in southern California got pissed when you gave them the brush off. These third-worlders just took it on the chin, extremely polite, then they nabbed you off the street, by limo no less. "All right old girl," she told herself, " let's just try and get some info, no panicking, and come up with a plan. If he wants me for a wife, surely they're not going to hurt me."

"Rusty, could you get me some ibuprofen and a bottle of water?"

"Amran," he called, snapping his fingers, and one of the men went forward, returning in just a second with the pills and a bottle of Perrier. Holly took three ibuprofens and drank the entire bottle of water. She had not paid much attention to the other men on the plane, but started trying to size them up now. They didn't look that tough or mean, more robotic. And she got the impression they didn't like Rusty that much. They just glared at him when he wasn't looking. They mostly seemed to be ignoring her now. Earlier, when she got on the plane, they were all sizing her up like she was some kind of an American artifact. She figured it was because of the Sri Lankan movie connection, but now she wasn't so sure. It didn't matter about them. Rusty was the herd boss here, the one to pump for information.

"So Rusty, where are we now?"

"That's a good question. I think we're headed up the west coast of Canada. From there we'll swing west over southern Alaska and then down the coastline of Russia to Seoul. We'll stop there. We should be landing in Colombo around lunch tomorrow."

"Where's Colombo?"

"Oh, uh, that's the capital of Sri Lanka."

"So why are we going so far north, and why to Seoul?"

"Sorry lady, I don't draw up the flight plans, but I assume it keeps the plane over land a lot more than flying over the ocean, and we've got to stop for fuel. This baby holds a lot, but it's still just an eight seater."

"I won't stay in Sri Lanka, not with that kidnapping bastard. You might as well let me out in Seoul. Or better yet, go get the pilot to turn around and go back to California."

Rusty broke out laughing. The veins in his thick neck were bulging, and to Holly he sounded like a pig squealing. "You'll stay in Sri Lanka. And you'll do and act as you're told." He leaned down over her again, his thick arms invading her personal zone, looking quite serious. "I don't think you've caught on. You will never see the States again. Your little rich bitch Hollywood actress life is over. You act right, and you will live a long, and I assure you, a very comfortable life. You fuck up, get disrespectful, cause a scene, or try to go away, and I assure you there will be an unfortunate accident. I tell you all this because Mr. Langdor will not. He will treat you with total respect, like he always has. You came over of your own accord and you love the man. Anything you do that betrays that image punches your ticket."

Now Rusty leaned in even closer. She could smell his boozy breath and see the ugly divots in his pig nose. He grabbed her hair with his big left paw and pulled her head back hard. She clenched her teeth in pain. "You will be watched, and you will be monitored twenty-four/seven. Just one glitch, one wink at the wrong person, and Mr. Langdor, your new husband, will be in mourning. And make no mistake, those are his orders, not mine. You're his ticket to be the next president. He figures you are good for a ton of votes hanging on his arm, and you know just how to play the part. So you better put on the performance of your life."

He let go of her head and walked back up to the cockpit. Holly let her head flop forward. She tried to breathe, but it was hard. "Oh my God," she thought. This was for real. She was scared now. She had never been this scared in her life. He wasn't kidding around. If she made a call, yelled out for help, or did anything but what Langdor wanted, she would be gone. They would find a way to cover it, make it look like some kind of accident. She was doomed to play this guy's wife until he didn't want her anymore or she made a mistake. She'd get bumped off sooner or later. Maybe right after he won that damned election Rusty mentioned. So the game was out. That was what it was all about. He wanted to get her out of California quick, before she started blabbing to people about her true feelings. And boy did it ever work out slick. All she had said to her friends was that he was a nice man and she was enjoying his company. That was the truth of it too. And everyone would buy it. She had done just enough screwball things in the past for people to buy it. She had been complaining for two years about the lousy parts she was getting. Everybody she was close to knew that she wasn't very happy with Hollywood anymore.

Old Holly just fell in love again. Ran off to live the good life with the rich President of Sri Lanka. That's what they would think. Rusty came back from up front.

"We're just about into Alaska now. By the way, you'll get the rest of the briefing in Colombo. Your passport and all of your clothes and other personal effects will be there within an hour of our arrival. You will have to make some phone calls as soon as we arrive. Your parents and your agent, to start with. You will be told what to say. Don't mess it up sweetie. I'd hate to see you miss your own wedding. I understand it's going to be one hell of a shindig."

"Damn them," she thought. They had this thing planned to the last detail.

They weren't just flying the long way around to be over land. That was bullshit. They had to get into her apartment to get all of her things. That would take time. Her things then had to be flown over and arrive close to when she did. Especially the passport. Now she wished she had kept it in a safe box with her Will, which she undoubtedly would be needing soon. But her passport was right there in her jewelry box. She was just helping out the bad guys left and right. Waltzed right onto this plane without one iota of duress; even signed an autograph in the terminal. That lucky old lady. The last autograph signed by the famous Holly Allen before she mysteriously ran away to play Grace Kelly. The damn thing would probably be worth a fortune in a year or two. Maybe a couple million on ebay, right after the car crash. Yep, just like Grace Kelly.

Holly started shaking. At first, she though it was just her nerves working her over, and then she realized it was the plane. The plane was shaking. Rusty was paying attention to it too. So were the other men. It was getting worse by the minute. Rusty finally got up and looked out the window over the wing.

"Ice," was all he said, and he took off to the cockpit. The pilot was cutting back on the throttle, and the vibration let up a little. In a minute, Rusty came back and the concern was written all over his face. "De-icer's not working. We're pretty coated and we're losing altitude. Damn it. I told him to check this thing out good. This jet has never been this far north. Hey guys, get buckled in good. You too, lady. Pilot says we're going to have to put down, airport or no. He's just trying to clear these big mountains and then we'll look for a strip of some kind. I'm going to go up front and help him look."

Holly looked out the window. She couldn't see far, but every few seconds she got a glimpse of a mountain top, a couple of them higher than the plane. Just what she needed: to die in a plane crash right before her next wedding.

They were dropping, and there was no doubt about it. Holly got her shoes on tight, cinched down her seat belt, bent forward and wondered what she had done to deserve all of this. The plane was shaking hard again. She looked out the window. The mountains seemed lower than before, so maybe they were about through them. Then Holly heard a grinding noise and thought the plane was breaking up. No, it was the landing gear. The pilot was putting the landing gear down. Thank

God. Maybe he had found a runway, or an airport. She knew an airport was unlikely, but she looked out the window again, looking for lights. There were none, but they were out of the mountains.

All of a sudden the jet started banking hard to the left. Holly looked out the left side window, but the plane was in such a hard roll that she was looking down into the ground. Then she heard the landing gear going back up. She was totally freaked out now. What in the hell was going on. "Just get it over with already," she whispered. Now she could see more out the window as the plane was easing out of the bank. It was the mountains again. He was flying this crippled jet right back into those mountains. She could feel the increase in power, the plane starting to shake violently.

The first impact slammed the left side of her face hard into the back of Rusty's empty seat. The seat belt almost cut her in two. Then she whipped backwards violently. The second time her head slammed forward she had the sensation of the plane being on water, bucking waves like a Sea-Doo in the surf. That was the last thing she remembered.

Chapter 10

DECISIONS

Ab was up at five. He couldn't sleep well knowing what he was up against. This really wasn't the sort of expedition a guy took off on with only four hours sleep. Bearman would just laugh at him. "Put the bullshit aside; just get it done; act like a man," he would say. Ab wasn't as worried about the fate of the plane people as he was about scaling that ridge and getting up on the ice. He didn't cause that plane to crash. He wouldn't take on any guilt about that. He would do the best he could to get on the ice and help. But this was a man-sized task on a warm sunny day. The weather would be bad today, and probably stay so for several days. It was nothing in this part of Alaska for the weather to turn off rotten and stay socked in for a week or two. Ab had seen hunters stuck in camp for an extra week waiting for the weather to break so a floatplane could get in. Which also meant there would be no air rescue today for potential survivors. And that was assuming anybody on the face of the earth besides him knew about it.

So the job fell on his shoulders, and he would do the best he could with it. He started a pot of coffee and put two chunks of poplar in the stove. It was a big black potbelly, and there were still coals from last night. Within a minute, the thing was huffing and puffing, sounding like a freight train. Ab closed the damper partway, poured himself a cup of coffee, and put a dip in his mouth. It was his one really nasty habit, but it relaxed him, and he always concentrated better with a dip in. What to pack was his problem. Decisions he made now may very well mean life or death later.

He took a look around the cabin. There were bunk beds, one of them with clothes, extra sleeping bags and rolled up tents on them. The other had an assortment of guns spread out on it like you would see on a display rug in a gun store. There were connibear traps on nails in the wall. Near the door were gore-tex coats, hats and overalls hanging on more nails. There was an old wooden table and four chairs. Candle holders with burned down candles sat on it, and the drippings of wax from years gone by were speckled all over it. There was a beat up deck of cards and his bottle of Jack on it too. Canned goods of all kinds lined the shelves of the back wall. Ab was seeing it all, but his mind was packing that pack, figuring out the triage—what to take, what to leave behind. He sat there for ten minutes, drinking two cups of coffee, spitting in the woodstove every minute or so. He grabbed his Dana pack and went to work. His Northface Mountain Tent went in first. It was a two man, but not very comfortable with two men in it. However, he could get four in there if he had to save lives.

Ab would bet his life on that tent, and had on a number of occasions. The thing would just laugh at sixty mile winds if it was set up properly. He always set it up properly. Next he stuffed in two down sleeping bags. If there were more folks, they'd just have to huddle up and share.

Ab's idea was that if he could get any survivors out of the weather and keep them relatively warm, he could get to Jatahmund Lake for help and probably be back on the second day. He put in two quart water bottles and a backpacking stove with three small cans of fuel. They'd need a way to melt ice for water. They would have to do without much food. He found a few bags of that freeze-dried crap and threw it in. It tasted like cardboard. So they would just have to live on cardboard and water for a few days.

Next he put in clothes. This stuff was bulky and took up a lot of pack space. Extra socks, long underwear, woolpants, and shirts. He tied two gore-tex jackets on the outside of the pack because it didn't matter if they got wet. Then he put two thermarests rolled together on bottom. He stuffed in a few other odds and ends and put the first aid kit in the top and cinched down all the compression straps. Now if he could just pick the fucker up.

If there was anybody alive, he hoped they had decent shoes. He couldn't haul assorted footwear up there. They probably didn't. They were most likely in smart business attire, never giving a thought to the what ifs in this world. Yul D went down on a chopper in '69 in Laos. He told Ab the story about a hundred times. He'd saved his own life by running through a bunch of burning shit, most of it under his feet. Smoked the soles right off his jump boots, but they kept his feet and ankles from burning up. Ab took the lesson to heart. He always wore good boots on an airplane.

He put on longjohns, wool socks, hiking pants, a gore-tex jacket and hiking boots. Then he thought about a gun. The .480 was just too much bulk and weight. He strapped on a Kimber 1911, cocked and locked, in a strong side Sparks leather holster, and put three extra magazines in mag pouches on his left side. He wouldn't leave the cabin without a sidearm. Yul D didn't raise any fools. That gave him thirty-three rounds on tap. A .45 was a little light for bears, but they'd have to wade through the brass to get him.

Ab shut down the woodstove, got his gloves and a tuque, and lugged the big pack up on his shoulder. "Had to be seventy pounds," he thought. It was still dark outside, and the cold felt good to him after being in the dry heat in the cabin. He tried to get a fix on the sky as he lugged the pack over to the four wheeler. It wasn't snowing yet, but the sky was fully overcast and the morning would be slate gray. It was cold and windy, probably in the mid-twenties. He bungied down the pack and filled the gas tank on the quad. He should be parked and climbing by daylight.

He couldn't remember what day it was, not even the day of the week. But it was getting on in September, and this far north, each successive day would be six or eight minutes shorter.

Chapter 11

COLD AND LONELY

Holly Allen was having another dream. In this one, she was in Sri Lanka somewhere, and it was brutally cold. Some men were standing over her. They had her strapped down in a chair, and the strap around her waist was too tight, hurting her stomach badly. One of the men was leaning over her, sticking pins in the side of her face. She dreamed it was some kind of Sri Lankan acupuncture, some voodoo ritual designed to brainwash her and keep her in line. The men were talking among themselves, and Holly tried to open her eyes to see who they were. Her left eye just wouldn't comply, but she got the right one squeaked open. She remembered now, the plane.

The pins in her face, as it turned out, was sleet hitting her. She felt her face, could barely put pressure on the left side, and then rubbed her hands through her hair. It was damp, but not soaking wet. Her feet were beyond cold, and when she tried to turn and look out of the fuselage, her stomach muscles just screamed at her. With one good eye, she surveyed her surroundings.

The jet, toward the front, was still in one piece. She could see toward the cockpit, but it was dark up in front. Behind her about five feet, there was no more plane. It was wide open. The tail was just gone. It had broken into in a jagged pattern. And wires and hoses hung all askew from the wall, insulation scattered about. It was like the plane was a twix bar that someone had snapped in two. She started trying to ease herself out of her seat, but was still strapped in. She got the belt off and eased herself up. She turned around and looked outside. It looked like it was getting daylight out, but everything looked the same. The sky, the ground, the air, it was all the same. The exact same grayish white color, like they had crashed into a cloud and were suspended in mid-air.

Holly tried to hobble out the back opening, but kept stumbling because a stiletto heel was missing from her right black pump. She heard talking and saw Rusty and Amran standing in the open. She caught something about 'dumping it in a crevasse,' when Rusty noticed her.

He and Amran stopped and stared at her. Then Rusty walked over to the plane. "Well," he said, "looks like everybody made it except for the pilot. Sort of a shame, too. He did one hell of a job setting this thing down. But then again, it's his fault we're in this god-damn mess. He should have had this thing checked out better."

"What happened?"

"We were going through those big mountains, and when we knew we were going down, we just tried to push on through them. As soon as we cleared them, we saw our problem. There was no flat ground. But we could see this big glacier off to the left, so we made a snap decision to turn around and try and hold enough altitude to slide across it." Rusty pointed back down the landing path, and Holly could see the effect, like a snow plow had driven from somewhere in the distance up to the back of the plane. "If we had dropped another twenty feet," he continued, "we'd all be greasy spots on a cliff wall right now. What saved us was pulling the gear back up. It was too much drag, pulling us down. So he turned, pulled it back up, and gave it full throttle. We made it by a cunt hair. The pilot broke his neck. He never strapped in, just forgot, too busy and all. Everybody else made it, just banged up like you. It was really a damn textbook emergency landing, til we got sideways. Then the rear hit something and snapped off. The front plowed into this snow bank, and the rear end just slid off in a big crevasse."

"So, what happens now?" Holly's teeth were chattering as she said it, and she had her arms wrapped around herself.

"You just get back on the plane." He said it like she was a problem, something to be dealt with in due course. Holly stumbled back in. In two days, her life had turned into one nightmare after another. But she was alive, and Alaska was closer to home than Sri Lanka. Like that made a difference. Sure, she'd just walk on down the Canadian coast in a pair of busted pumps and a beige skirt. "Hey, it *was* wool," she thought. Maybe stop off in Vancouver and see a few old friends.

Warmth was what she needed. She had to get something on her feet. She started rummaging toward the front of the plane, opening compartments. The first one had three blankets in it, the next one a first-aid kit. Inside the kit she found a plastic handled scalpel. Under the bar there was a roll of twine and two cases of Perrier water, cases of Diet Coke, and other mixers. Holly gathered all this stuff up and sat down in a seat. She drained two bottles of water and then opened a can of Diet Coke and took a sip. Then she took the scalpel and cut two three-foot squares from a blanket. She dumped the pumps, wrapped one of the blanket squares around her left foot, took the plastic cover from a case of Perrier and tied it up good with the twine, then did the same with the other foot. She held up the other two blankets, studied them, and cut arm holes in one. Then she cut a seatbelt off, put the blanket on and tied it around her waist. The other one she used as a shawl. She was warming up now, which was making the pain in her stomach and face worse. She found the ibuprofen and took three more. With her new outfit on, she went back up to the bar area and checked out the food supply. There were some soggy looking sandwiches in plastic wrapping. The microwave didn't work, so she ate one cold with a bag of potato chips. It was actually pretty good. She hadn't eaten since yesterday at lunch.

Reality was hitting her square in the face again. If there was any rescue mission coming, which was doubtful, these boys weren't going to let her come along and spill her guts about a kidnapping. No, she had to be dealt with. It was just like last night. It was just a matter of time, and the ax would fall. Then it hit her—the crevasse. Holly Allen's grave was going to be cold and lonely.

Chapter 12

THE CLIMB

Ab couldn't remember being this out of breath in a long time. It was daylight now, probably eight o'clock. This far north, the sun didn't really rise in the east and set in the west; it just kind of circled overhead. But there would be no sun today, and the snow was coming down now. He turned around and plopped down on his ass. He had been walking now for an hour on land so steep going up the drainage that he always seemed to be looking into the ground at his next step. As he caught his breath, he looked out across the low rolling hills to the north. It was like an oil painting—maybe like one of those Kincaid paintings. The view was rich in color, with all the bright fall colors in the rolling hills below. The snowfall muted it all down, giving the day a pastoral feel, warm and fuzzy if you were in an art gallery looking at it all on a canvas. Ab had been in a Kincaid art gallery once in New York City. He was following his wife around, bored, but dutiful, a man woefully out of place on a vacation shopping spree. He looked up and saw a huge painting and recognized it at once. "Mount Rundle," he said. A lady came up behind him, clanking from too much jewelry, and said, "Ah, you know Mr. Kincaid's work."

"Nope, I never heard of him. I just know Mount Rundle." She was a store clerk. She just looked at him, obviously confused. Then he caught on. She didn't know it was a real place.

"It's outside the town of Banff. In Alberta, Canada." He looked back up at the huge painting. It was beautiful; the guy obviously knew his stuff. "He got it right," Ab said. He looked at the price tag, four thousand dollars.

"We can ship it anywhere you like, sir." Ab's wife walked up. "That'll be the day when Ab Bailey spends four grand on a painting." Ab didn't have the wife anymore, but the painting sat over the fireplace in his cabin in Lowndes County.

He couldn't make out the quad now. The snow was getting too heavy. He pushed himself back up, feeling every ounce of the heavy pack. It took two more hours to get to the top of the drainage and now, on rubbery legs, he had to face his old enemy. Three hundred yards of a two-foot slippery ledge, five hundred feet of freefall your reward for a misstep. He took a five-minute break, tried to steel his nerves, and stepped out onto it. Balance was his problem, the big pack wanting to pull over backwards with every step. He almost went over twice, the second time only saving himself by spinning sideways and dropping to his knees. He couldn't keep the sweat out of his eyes, and the narrow walkway was as slick as hoot owl shit. But he made it. And thank God, Bearman's rope still hung down from the top of the glacier. He got his right hand on the rope and felt an immediate sense of relief. He turned sideways and carefully eased off the big pack. After almost four hours with the thing on, he now felt like a spaceman, damn near weightless.

Ab always thought fat people should be made to carry a pack all day that weighed that much. Then, when they took it off, they would feel light as a feather for a while. That way, they could get a grasp on how they would feel if they really got rid of sixty or seventy pounds of fat. But if you marched them out across this ledge there would just be a lot of fat corpses down below.

Ab found the plastic case Bearman stored behind a rock last year. He got out one of the ropes and two of the carabiners that were in the case. He tied one end to a carabiner and snapped it on the pack carry loop. He tied the other end of the rope through his belt. He hooked the other carabiner on his belt and wound the existing rope on it. He put almost all his body weight on the rope and tugged. Hope this baby holds, he thought. If it broke and he fell, after he passed the ledge, the other rope would yank the pack down after him. So he would slam into the rocks below, and a second later the seventy-pound pack would hammer him. He was glad no one was around to see it because it sure would look stupid. Ab started up the rocks, nervous as hell the whole way, but it only took about fifteen minutes to reach the top. The rope had held. He shook the nerves off and immediately started looking for the plane. "Damn it," he said aloud. He didn't see a thing. The snow was coming on now, but he could see up the glacier for several hundred yards. He looked back over the ledge. Getting the pack on top was the hard part. Pulling up dead weight, and he was already exhausted. It took ten minutes to get it up and over the ledge. As soon as he had it on, he started moving again. He was eager to find this thing, find out what happened.

This finger of the glacier was over a thousand yards from end to end. It ran slightly uphill from the drop off where Ab climbed on it. The high end backed into another mountain with high snowdrifts that rolled down and eventually formed the ice, which continually, over thousands of years, worked its way north to the ledge. The melt off each year ran into several drainages, one of them being the headwaters of Snag Creek, and eventually dumped into the Chisana River below.

This finger of the glacier was as wide as it was long, so Ab started angling southwest, looking out ahead as he went, trying to see some part of the wreckage or cut its track where it had plowed the ice. It didn't take long. The runway became obvious. Two feet deep and fifteen feet wide. He started following alongside it while looking ahead every minute or so. Seven hundred yards and still no plane. But he was on track. He found two hunks of sheet metal about halfway up. Other than that, the thing had just stayed on course, but where was the plane? The snow had really picked up now and visibility was down to about seventy-five yards. Almost to the base of the bigger mountain, Ab heard voices. People were alive.

Chapter 13

THE ARRIVAL

Holly was aware that Rusty had been having private conferences with the other men all morning. They mostly stayed outside. She knew they were all five as cold as she was. Two of the younger men had come in earlier and gone to the cockpit. She could hear them arguing in a foreign language. They came back a few minutes later, each one carrying some of the dead pilot's clothes. A little later Rusty came on the plane.

"It's starting to snow pretty good out there. Me and two of these other boys are going to scale this mountain we bumped into and try to get a fix on how to get down off this glacier. Amran will take care of you." That same tone of voice again. "Yeah, he's going to take care of me," she thought, looking up at Rusty with her good eye. That's when she noticed the gun. Slung over his shoulder was a black military looking rifle, short, with a rectangular curved thing hanging out of the bottom. It had a funny, space-age looking sighting system on top.

Holly hated guns. Everybody in the circle she ran in hated guns. They hated what guns stood for. They hated the NRA. Only policemen and soldiers should have guns. Especially not thugs like Rusty. "Are you going to shoot me with that?"

"Don't be foolish. We'll be back in a few hours. Maybe we'll have something figured out."

Holly covered up with the blanket and dozed off in the seat for a while. It was quiet, with only the snow falling outside. Occasionally, she would hear Amran and the other man talking in a foreign language, sometimes arguing, sometimes chanting.

Holly was having those half-awake, half-asleep dreams, the bad ones. The problem was, every time she woke up, reality was even worse—unlike at home where you could shake them off and go to the coffee pot and get on with your real life. Her real awake life now was nothing but the cold and the impending doom that would come when they decided it would. Helplessness, Holly thought. It had to be one of the most miserable places a person could be. Without an alternative, without hope, and without any skills to rise above the problem and defeat it and get away. So Holly just sat there, trying to stay bundled up and warm, and softly cried.

In days to come she knew she would be even more famous than she was now. But she would be dead, and all her fame would be for naught. And it wouldn't be a good fame. Just the memory of a few stupid movies, television shows, three bad marriages, and the dumb choices she had made in the last week of her life.

Holly had seen the admiring, emulating faces of young girls looking at her over the years. The adoring fans who wanted to be like her, or even to be her. Girls who were like her when she was young, wanting that lifestyle, all the glamour and the attention. It all looked good on the surface, but late at night when the doors were all closed and the cameras went away, you remain a human being with a real life to live, and real problems to face. And that was where Holly Allen felt like a complete failure—in the living department. The amazing part was that she probably handled the real life stuff better than most of her counterparts. Hollywood was littered with wrecked female lives. Drugs and booze were the norm. People didn't take those drugs and drink that booze to deal with the fame; they did it to escape the other side of the coin—the person that was really inside; not the celluloid version.

So Holly just sat on the cold wrecked plane and went through her life piecemeal. All the good things, all the bad. She was at the end, and the ledger just didn't tally up right. It was too lopsided in the wrong direction. The bad items on the list were really bad, and the good ones were transparent, only looking good on the surface. Maybe that had been her problem all along. But what was inside? What had really been accomplished? Soon enough, she thought, none of that would matter. So Holly sat, curled up in a crouch on a wrecked jet in the middle of Alaska, and did the slow version of her life flashing before her eyes. It didn't make a very pretty movie.

About two hours after Rusty and the other two left, Amran came on the plane grinning.

"Please come outside," he said. Well, this was probably it. Dead woman walking. She felt more like a cavewoman walking, with her new boots and her blanket dress. She stumbled outside and noticed how hard it was snowing. Amran and a smaller man got up close to her now, and she could see it in their eyes. They were going to kill her. The smaller man walked up to her. Suddenly, he hit her hard across the face, and she fell straight into the snow. The pain almost made her black out. She got up on her hands and knees, and she could see blood dripping from her mouth into the white snow. Amran was yelling at the other man. "No, not here, over by the crevasse. We can't have blood here. If someone comes for us, there will be questions." The smaller man said something in a different language, and she could see Amran shaking his head yes. "But do it quickly," he said. "It is wrong, though. You should not do that with an infidel. Make it quick, cut her throat, and dump her in the crevasse. Cover up the blood with snow."

That was it. She would be raped and murdered. She didn't feel any fear. She just felt hollow, already dead. They stopped talking and both looked around the corner of the wrecked plane. Holly looked over with her good eye. It looked like a man. He had long brown hair, his right hand on his hip, with an intense stare that looked as cold as the landscape she was hugging.

Chapter 14

OFF THE ICE

Ab could see the half plane now, guided to it by the voices. With six more inches of snow, you could do twenty flybys in a cub on a sunny day and never see it. The back of the plane had simply disappeared, probably slid off in the big crevasse to the west. The front had buried into the snow bank at the base of the higher peak. When Ab was ten yards from the wreckage, he could understand what he was hearing. Foreign accents, one man speaking English, the other some Hindi dialect. The man speaking English was saying something about doing it quick and something about infidels. It bothered Ab, the word infidel. It made him think of 9/11 and terrorists. This was a pretty unlikely place to meet a terrorist. But Ab Bailey was a cautious man. He slipped off his pack, unzipped his coat and got a good firing grip on the .45. Then he heard the clincher, "Make it quick, cut her throat, and dump her in the crevasse."

He came around the corner of the wreckage and let himself be seen. They both stopped what they were doing, and he could see the look of disbelief on their faces. He immediately saw the long knife in the smaller man's hands, and a small woman on her hands and knees, bleeding from the mouth. She looked up at him with help me written all over her face. Half of her face was attractive, the other half swollen and purple.

Ab focused on the larger man now, particularly on his hands. He had taught it in defensive handgun classes a hundred times. Forget about the face. No one can hurt you with a dirty look. Always watch the hands. And the hands were moving. Slowly at first, and then the right hand had swept the man's coat and Ab could see the frame of the gun, sitting high in a Kydex holster. For Ab Bailey, it was the point where muscle memory took over. He had shot IPSC and IDPA for years, a master class shooter in both sports.

The big man never even cleared the gun. Ab was too fast. He didn't even need a timer for this. At seven yards, with a good firing grip, he knew what it was. Somewhere around a half second with another two tenths for the double tap. All he had needed was to see the gun.

Once that mental trigger was tripped, he was on autopilot. He felt the first shot break, and from 300,000 rounds of rhythm and timing, had the second one out of the barrel the same nanosecond the gun was back in battery and out of recoil. His eyes had already broken to the smaller man, as he could see the ragdoll effect happening to the first. The small man was charging and screaming now, having let go of the woman. Dumbass, bringing a knife to a gunfight. Ab broke three shots in under a half second, calling them all good hits. He didn't even need the third one, just fired it out of meanness. The man was already on the ground, plowing up snow. "Cocksucker, gonna cut up a poor woman," Ab muttered.

Ab didn't holster his gun. He leveled it back and forth at the two men in the snow. Let 'em bleed on out, he thought. He scanned all around him, front and back, in case there were others. When he felt safe, he reached back with his left hand, pulled out a fresh mag, and switched it with the one in the gun, topping it off. He put the partial mag in his coat pocket. The entire fight, from the time he started his draw until the fifth shot was fired, was under a second and a half. Yul D said it all the time, "Two seconds is a lifetime in a gunfight." The woman was looking up at him now, one eye wide open, the other swollen shut. She was in shock, he could tell. And what in the hell was she wearing. He walked over, squatted down in the snow, and spit out some tobacco juice. She looked down at the brown hole it had made in the snow and then looked back up at him, the man who had saved her life.

"Howdy, Pocohantas. You got any other friends out here?"

Holly couldn't say anything. She just looked into the man's intense blue eyes. Where had he come from? Just appeared out of nowhere, and gunned down two men faster than she could blink her one good eye. Finally, she could get words out. "That, that was so fast."

"Could have been faster," Ab said. "If I'd had on a competition rig." He looked over at the two dead men, blood seeping out into the snow. "Guess it was fast enough. I think you got some splainin' to do."

"Help me up, please. Let's go in the plane for a second so I can sit down." Ab got Holly to her feet and they went inside. He looked around the inside. "All the comforts of home. So what about it, anybody else around?" Ab was walking through the plane, giving it the once over. Holly gave him the three minute condensed version of the last week of her life. Ab stopped, put his thumb in his mouth, bit down, thought about it for a minute and said, "These other three, do they have weapons?"

"One of them does, the big white guy. I don't know about the other two."

"Handgun or rifle?"

"Rifle. But not a hunting rifle. More like an army type gun. It was short and black, with stuff hanging off of it."

"Probably an AR."

"What's an AR?" Holly asked.

"Never mind. Think you can walk a few miles?"

"I'll try. I'd do anything to get away from here. And thank you. Thank you for helping me."

"No problem, lady. Double homicides are my specialty." He blew air out of his mouth and gave her that hard stare, the one he had on his face when she first saw him. "I just hope you're on the up and up." Ab walked back out and did a long search and scan. Depending on how far away these other three were when he fired, they might have heard it and been on the way back. Hopefully they were too far and the snow might have contained the sound somewhat. It was falling even harder now as Ab retrieved his backpack. He had to get this woman properly dressed and get a move on. He had a decision to make. Which way to go. He turned it over in his head several times. There was just no way. He couldn't get her down that vertical wall. End of story. He didn't even want to face that ordeal again. So there was only one way. They would go down the Klein Creek drainage to the southeast and hook back to the north and pick up the winter trail to the Canadian border, and come back into Carden Lake from the east. The only problem was it might take several days on foot, and Ab had never been that way, only seen it on the map.

He got her dressed in longjohns, wool pants, and two pairs of wool socks. The smaller man's boots were still a little too big, but it was the best they could do. Damn, she had good looking legs. She put on a big fleece lined shirt he had brought and one of the gore-tex jackets.

Ab pilfered through the plane, but didn't find much of value other than some coffee until he got to the liquor cabinet. Glory be to God, a bottle of Jack Daniels. The seal wasn't even cracked. This was weight he could afford to haul, essential survival gear. For good measure, he also threw in his pack the two bottles of merlot he found. Too bad none of these guys were dippers. He grabbed a can of coffee and then turned to Holly.

"You about ready?"

"I guess so." She didn't look too confident.

"Now, listen. If what you said is true, this guy has pretty much got to take you out. If you're dead, and he can get out of these mountains, he's home free. And from the way you described him, he's probably ex-military and he'll know how to survive out here. It's not that cold yet. All he's got to do is shoot a little food every couple of days and keep a good fire going at night. So we need to move hard, hard as we can. If that rifle is an AR, it's good to about 300 yards, maybe 400, depending on what kind of optics he's got on top. I'll be lucky to hit one of them past fifty with this 1911, so we gotta move fast, at least until we get to treeline. And until then, we gotta check our six a lot."

"Whatever you say, I'm with you." 1911's, AR's, checking sixes. She didn't understand a word of that stuff.

Ab came out of the plane first, looking hard in all directions. He got his bearings and headed southeast. There was five or six hours of daylight left. The snow wouldn't let up, but he had a compass out, keeping their line straight. He turned around every fifty yards to check their backtrail. It was obvious she couldn't keep up with him, even with the full pack on his back.

He would stop and wait on her while surveying the glacier. Visibility was under a hundred yards now, and for once in his life he was glad of it. When you're a hunter, you hate it, but when you're being hunted, it's pretty good stuff. Now he knew how the old bull moose felt.

He pushed her hard for three hours until it was obvious she was struggling.

"Why don't we take a little break. I think we'll be off the ice in about an hour. We got about two hours of daylight, and I'm hoping we'll find that Klein drainage pretty quick."

Holly was too tired to talk for a minute. Ab handed her a water bottle. "Drink all this you can. I don't need you dehydrating on me." She drank for a minute, then caught her breath.

"We'll freeze to death tonight," she said.

"No, we'll be fine if we don't get shot, or maybe eaten by bears."

"Great," she thought. That was all she needed. Survive a kidnapping. Survive a plane crash. Survive a throat cutting, and then get eaten by a bear.

Ab pushed on again and within an hour they were off the glacier. The ice had been fairly level, only sloping gradually down hill. The drainage was much steeper, with water running down the middle of it. Holly didn't get much of a view down hill because the snow was still coming down hard.

Ab felt better. This drainage was only half as steep as Snag Creek, with no cliffs or drop offs. He started looking for a flat spot down below, some place he could set up the tent. They lost altitude quickly. Within a half mile, they were getting into vegetation. Holly finally grabbed Ab and stopped him.

"I just can't go much farther. I'm sorry." Ab studied her face. There was half of an obviously beautiful woman standing in front of him. She was breathing hard and he could tell it was difficult for her to breathe out of her left nostril. It was almost swollen shut, as was her left eye. Walking hard was surely not good for it. Her hair was brown, about the same color as his and almost as long, but it was matted and sticking to her head. She was slumping at the shoulders from fatigue and stress, and with the outfit she had on, she just looked like a homeless person, down on her luck. If he had met her on a city street, he would have been reaching for a dollar bill.

"Don't be sorry. You're tougher than most of the hunters I've drug through these mountains," Ab said. He looked up and studied the sky. It was still snowing from the northwest, but the light was fading now, maybe thirty minutes til dark. He knew the temperature was dropping, but it was hard to tell when you were on the move, generating heat. He looked farther down the drainage, trying to find something. There was a rock wall just below, easy to walk around and get by, and Ab hoped the low side was flat. "I think I've found it." He took off again and in five minutes was dropping the heavy pack on the ground, studying the layout.

"This'll do. A little grass, a rock wall behind us to hide the tent and keep the snow off of us and break the wind. We got running water within twenty yards. They'd have to walk within ten feet of us in the dark to see us, and that ain't likely." It was the first Holly had heard of a tent. During the entire forced march, her greatest fear had been sleeping out on the cold ground tonight. She never wanted to wake up as cold as she had this morning. "What do you want me to do?"

Ab already had the two thermarests unrolled. He put them on the grass and up against the rock wall. "I want you to sit down right here and relax. Just leave everything else to old Ab."

"Is that your name, Ab?" That was the first time Ab realized they had not even been introduced. He was pulling a down sleeping bag out of a stuff sack. He unzipped it and took it over to the wall and spread it over Holly's arms, legs, and shoulders.

Another surprise. This guy was prepared, Holly thought. The down bag was like instant warmth. With all the stress and cold from the previous day, now sitting there warm, with a protector, Holly started to relax. She could feel the anxiety draining from her body. Ab stuck his hand out.

"Ab Bailey at your service. Resident dragon slayer and damsel in distress rescuer. And who might you be?"

Holly shook his hand. "I'm Holly Allen. Most distressed damsel you've ever met."

Ab rubbed his forehead and looked at the rock wall for a moment. "Holly Allen," he thought. That sounded familiar to him. "Well, Miss Holly, you just take it easy there and I'll get this camp set up and we'll have some cardboard and water for supper. Might even have a shot of grog. Sorry we can't have a fire this evening, but I can't risk it. Nothing to burn around here anyway. If we can get through tonight and tomorrow and make it down into the low bush, I'll get some proper food and we'll hide out where we can have a white man's fire."

Who was this guy, Holly wondered. Strange man, talked funny. Holly watched Ab set up the tent. He was meticulous about it. Pulling it taut, stretching out guy wires and moving the tent stakes around. It had stopped snowing now, and Ab had pulled off his coat. He wasn't a big man, but lean and well built. He moved smoothly and efficiently. Attention to detail, confidence—that was what this guy was all about. He was handsome too. Mostly it was the intensity in those blue eyes and the wildness in them. But he was in part a wildman. A man not a man to be taken lightly. He had proven that in the first five seconds she laid eyes on him. She was sure he had some stories to tell, and this would be one of them.

Ab went over to the creek and filled the two water bottles, came back and started rummaging through the top of his pack. He fished out two candy bars, two bags of peanuts, and two tin cups. He dug down deeper and came up with the whiskey bottle.

"I'd say it is the cocktail hour, Holly. What do you think?"

"Sounds good to me." He handed her a bag of peanuts and a candy bar. "Appetizers," he said. "Although I'm afraid supper won't be too appetizing." He cracked open the JD, poured some into the two cups, and sat down beside Holly on the other thermarest. It was dark now, the temperature dropping, but she was warm as a bug in a rug with the sleeping bag draped around her. Ab was sitting there with no coat or sleeping bag. "Aren't you cold?" she asked.

"I'm about to start the old woodstove from the inside." He poured some water into Holly's cup and then into his. "Damn it," he said.

"What's wrong?"

"I forgot to get any blue ice. Walked on that shit for six hours and never chipped off a bit. Oh well, this creek water was blue ice about three hours ago, but it won't be the same." It was still good. Whiskey was always at its best when you were tired and worn out from a hard day afield. They both had two pretty stiff drinks and then Ab got out the small stove and started boiling water. They shared the freeze-dried beef stroganoff from the same pot and it really wasn't as bad as Ab thought it would be. It was hot, and they were hungry, and that's what counted.

Ab would take a bite, then blow in and out and curse because it was so hot. "So you fell in love with this guy from Sri Lanka. Then he has the tough guy kidnap you, then the plane crashes in Alaska. That's a pretty wild tale. I wouldn't think Alaska was on the way from L.A. to Sri Lanka. You guys just taking the scenic route, or what?"

"I was not in love with him. This was going to be our third date. We hadn't even kissed. I told him I wouldn't see him after the last date. Anyway, he said he was going home. I was just trying to be nice, and I got kidnapped for it."

"You hadn't even kissed. I thought everybody in L.A. had sex thirty minutes after they met."

"That's not very nice."

"Sorry about that," he said. He took another bite of the stroganoff. "So that was pretty careless, wasn't it? Just hopping on board a private plane with people you don't really know."

"I know that now."

"So anyway, why was this guy, what's his name, Langdor, so mesmerized with you?"

"Well, I'm an actress, and apparently, I'm pretty well known in Sri Lanka. So he was going to use me to help him win an election."

Ab squinted and tried to look at her close in the dark. That was it. He did know the name. He had seen this woman on TV before. He thought about it for a minute, then snapped his fingers. "Were you in that movie, the one where this guy steals the computer codes for the missile silos and sells them to the terrorists?"

"That was me."

"I'll be damn. That was a pretty good show. Except for the gunfights. They always suck. Not even close to realistic."

"That's because nobody in Hollywood knows anything about guns. We don't know anything, except that they're evil." Then she thought about it for a minute. "Well, not your gun."

Ab laughed. "Yeah. When they're saving your ass they're not too bad, are they? A gun's just a tool, Holly. It's like a hammer or a car. You leave a car sitting in the driveway, it'll never run over anybody. You put a drunk guy behind the wheel, you got a problem. I could leave my .45 laying on a rock out here for a thousand years, and it would never hurt a soul. People are the problem, not guns."

"I guess so. But if nobody had them. . . ."

"Look, you can't go back and uninvent something. I mean, I didn't make the world. I just have to live in it. So my idea is, I'm gonna have a weapon on and I'm gonna know how to use it, but only for the right reasons. No honest man has anything to fear from me. Your personal security is really up to you. You should know that by now."

What he said made sense to her. She thought about it. Anyone of a thousand guys she knew in Hollywood could have walked up on her by that plane, and they would both be lying in the bottom of a crevasse right now. But that was too much to contemplate this evening. Ab was there. She could rest now. The warmth of the sleeping bag, and the alcohol and food were working their magic. She was getting sleepy now. The stress, cold and exertion had taken their toll. "I might have to lay down soon."

Ab got up and got the first aid kit out of the pack. "Let's get you cleaned up first."

The man was so gentle. He washed her face, then carefully dabbed ointment on the cut on her mouth. Then he heated some water and took her shoes and socks off. He held a small flashlight in his mouth and inspected her feet. "Just a couple of small blisters. We'll put something on those in the morning." Then he washed her feet, gently, with warm water, massaged them a bit, and put her socks back on. He got her up with her sleeping bag and ground pad and helped her in the tent. "Keep your clothes on and use these others for a pillow. Zip that bag up tight." She couldn't help herself. She pulled him down and kissed him on the lips. She just had so much gratitude for this man. He had no reason to help her except for decency. He was a decent man. It seemed odd to kiss him, but it was the only way she had to show her appreciation and give back some of the warmth she was getting from him.

"Wow," Ab said. "Go to sleep. You're going to need all your strength tomorrow. I'm going to stay up a while—make sure we're alone." Holly drifted off within five minutes.

Ab put on his coat, sat down and poured himself another drink. Even her feet were pretty, he thought.

Chapter 15

RUSTY'S LUCK

Rusty had gone up the west side of the buttress and sent one of the other men south and one east. It was a hard climb. Just rock and ice. But he had climbed before, and the other men were younger and in good shape. He gave them specific instructions—they were looking for the easiest way off the glacier. A walkdown, if possible. He knew from the landing that going north wouldn't work because they came in over a sheer cliff. It would be east, south or west. He doubted west would work because of the crevasse the plane's tail section had gone into. But southwest might be a possibility. It was tough going. Without gloves, he kept stopping to warm his hands.

The damn snow wasn't helping anything either. Visibility was getting worse instead of better. Climbing was so frustrating. Every time he thought he was getting to the top, another higher summit would poke its head up. It took almost two hours, but he was getting a feel for the topography. The glacier was fingered, with the smallest one being the one they landed on. To the south, the mountain dropped off, but he could see even larger peaks looming in the distance. That was out. The crevasse to the west hooked on around the mountain he was on and had large peaks on the other side of it as well. So west or southwest wouldn't work. The glacier's largest finger was the one going east. It looked like a gentler descent, but it was hard to say with so much snow falling. He could only see a portion of it from his side of the mountain, but Shinda, the man he sent east, should have a much better view.

Rusty would wait to make a decision until he compared notes with the other two, but he was sure they would be heading south and east in the morning. The AR was frustrating to carry, but he didn't know this country. Might be grizzlies or polar bears up here. He didn't know. A .223 wasn't his first choice for bear defense, but it was what he had. Shinda had one too; the other man a nine millimeter beretta, just about big enough for rabbits.

Rusty sat down for a rest break before heading back down. It wouldn't take as long going down. He drank the bottle of water he had in his pocket and tossed it onto the rocks. One more night on the glacier. They would huddle up in the plane tonight and leave at daylight. It wasn't brutally cold, but it would be a miserable night. It was too bad about the woman, but it couldn't be helped. She was expendable at this point. Amran knew what to do. He'd pass the chore off. That evil little helper of his would like it. He loathed Americans. He would have set off bombs all over L.A. if Rusty had cut him loose. He'd probably use that nasty knife he was always whetting.

If anybody asked, she died in the crash. Went over with the tail section. Such a tragedy. A wonderful woman. Yes, they had gotten close in their short time together. So sad, so sad. He even instructed the others to tell Langdor that they lost her in the crash, if they ever got back. Rusty didn't need any more complications in his life than he already had. He'd learned it way back when in special forces: KISS, or keep it simple stupid. That was back in the good old days, just drinking beer at night and training to fight all day. And then that fucking NCO bitch squealed and he got court martialed for rape. Six years in the brig and a dishonorable. Fuck 'em all. He couldn't get anything going in the States after that. Ended up in India doing some contract security work and then hooked up with Langdor, a man on a mission. That guy was going to be President of Sri Lanka or bust a nut one. Anyway, Rusty had a pretty cushy gig now. Just knocking down some of those crazy Tamil Tiger gangs when they got out of hand around the estate. Nothing he couldn't handle in his sleep.

Handling things was what Rusty had learned to do years ago. Some people went to pieces when bad things happened to them. Other people were able to go on, and even keep a good disposition about things. But Rusty was the third kind. He was the guy who could handle it, but only with a monster dose of bitterness thrown in. He was the man who went cold and bad.

For Rusty, that started right after Desert Storm. He left a beautiful wife and three-month-old son behind to do his country's bidding, and he was proud to do it. The thanks he got was a wife who had an affair while he was gone. Then she up and left with the baby for a man who ran a landscaping business. Rusty spent every dollar of his combat pay on a lawyer to help get his son back. But the soft, feminist judge disagreed. A baby belonged with its mother, even if she was a cheating whore. The child would be in a much more healthy environment in the landscaping world that with a father who killed people in wars.

That was the final straw for Rusty. For doing his duty he not only got no respect from his ungrateful country or his wife or the legal system, but instead he got raped. They put him in jail for rape, but they got it backwards. He had made up his mind the day he got out. From now on, it would be death before dishonor. And he didn't mean his own death.

Rusty heard the shots in the distance. Two fast ones, followed by three more. That stupid fuck Amran, he couldn't hit shit. Didn't matter, it was over, she was history now.

He started back down the mountain. Now that the woman problem was tidied up, it was just a matter of getting back to civilization. Find a town, a store, something. He wished he knew more about Alaska. He did know that the Alaska Highway came into the state from the southeast corner and ran northwest. So they would have to hook north and east at some point. Surely, if they got in the lower areas, they could cut a trail or a road within a day or two. He didn't want to be out here any longer than he had to. He could do it; he knew how. The worst part would be putting up with those other four morons. They were always quiet, almost reserved around people they didn't know. But you get them off by themselves, or just with him, and they would start fighting and turn into a bunch of screaming banshees. They were hard to understand too. They'd be speaking English one minute, then Sinhala, then Tamil, sometimes all in the same sentence.

Rusty caught up with Shinda and Doran, the other man, about a half mile from the plane. They were just sitting on the rocks up over the glacier, neither one out of breath.

"Well, what about it?"

"South is no good," Doran said. "Sheer dropoffs, and then higher and higher mountains.

"Yeah, that's what I thought. What about the east?" He looked at Shinda.

"Not sure. The glacier goes a long way, but there was so much snow. I didn't see any high mountains that way."

"Well, that's it then. We'll follow the glacier down that way til we get off or have to jump, cause one more night is all I'm staying up here." Both the other men were nodding their heads in agreement. "Let's go see if those two knuckleheads got enough snow piled up to knock some of the wind out of the back of the plane. I bet they haven't done shit."

It took another forty-five minutes to get off the base of the mountain and back to the plane. Doran was twenty yards ahead of Shinda, and Rusty was bringing up the rear. Doran let out a blood curdling Sinhala scream, and Shinda took off running. Then he was screaming too. Rusty racked a round into the chamber of his AR and came around the fuselage at low ready and saw the bodies. Doran was squalling now, as the smaller man was his brother.

"Fuck. What in the hell?" Rusty leaned the rifle up against the plane. "Where's the woman. Find the woman." But it was no use. They were basket cases now. Breaking out in idiotic chants and crying. He went around the plane and looked as far as he could in every direction. Nothing. Didn't see a thing. He went over to the small body and pushed Doran out of the way. There was one hole through the nose that had come out the back of the neck. A shot angling downward. He pulled the shirt open. Two puckered wounds. One dead center of the left nipple, the other a bit higher and four inches right. Rigor mortis had already set in, the arms and legs already cock stiff. He went over to Amran. Same story. Two holes, three inches apart, dead level. Amran's nine was missing.

Doran got in his face. "We go. We go now. Find this bitch, cut her throat." He was screaming.

Rusty knocked him down. "That's not all you'll find, you fucking moron. She ain't alone."

Shinda didn't get it either. "She took Amran's gun. She shot them. She can only be out there alone. I vote with Doran. We go now and cut her throat."

"This ain't a fucking democracy, Shinda. And unless she had a .45 hid in her crotch, she didn't shoot anybody. Them ain't 'nine' holes."

Something had caught Doran's eye. He reached down in the snow and picked it up. Rusty took it from him. ".45 brass." He tossed it at Shinda.

Rusty went on the plane and made a gin and tonic for himself. There was some water and booze left, but just a few things to eat. He thought it through. He had no idea how somebody got up here, but it really didn't matter now. This had just turned into a big game hunting trip. Whoever it was, that woman would be blabbing her head off to them, unless. He went back out. "Shinda, Doran. Look for any tracks. They might already be covered, but look anyway. See if there's two sets or one.

"I thought you said there was someone else," Shinda said.

"Yeah, but I was thinking, maybe we got lucky, and Amran had already offed her before he managed to get himself shot. Not likely, but it sure would be convenient for us."

Doran found the tracks, mostly snowed in, but there were clearly two sets, headed southeast. It was getting dark now, and it would be suicide to head out across the ice in it.

They had gone back to chanting again. "All right, boys, get your prayer vigil over with, and get some sleep. We got to move like hell tomorrow. Get this thing over with." Besides, he didn't want to hear any more of that gibberish.

Chapter 16

KLEIN CREEK

Ab finished his drink, stood up, and took a long leak. He listened in the dark for a couple more minutes, but all he heard was the water rolling downhill into the Klein Creek. He was hoping this guy Holly had described wasn't one of those "ninja delta we own the night" fuckers. He might wake up with his throat cut. He put the thought down. Highly unlikely. Anyway, he couldn't keep hauling her downhill all night. Let her rest. He'd be up at daylight and get her moving quick, right after he had his coffee and a dip.

He gathered up his stuff and put it in the tent. She was breathing those hard deep breaths of someone who had gone to sleep totally exhausted. Gone to the world. He got in his bag and reached his arm over to see if she was all inside of hers. He felt an arm out, and started trying to put it back in her bag, and it flopped over him and hugged him tight. He might get used to this. Ab dozed off quickly, tired from the day's events.

He slept past daylight. He knew it as soon as his eyes opened. He checked his throat, and then gave Holly her arm back. He laced up his boots, grabbed his .45, still cocked and locked, and got out of the tent. He eased around the rock wall and peered up the drainage. Nothing. By the time the water was boiling he heard her stirring around, getting her boots on.

She got out, walked over and kissed him again, then sat down against the wall.

"That's the most I've been kissed in the last year. I should shoot more people. Here, drink some coffee and have a candy bar. It's the last one." He got up and checked up the drainage again. "I want to be moving again in fifteen minutes." She didn't feel like it, but she would do it. Her stomach muscles were hurting more now, and the swelling was not going down in her face. Her legs felt like rubber. "Ready when you are," she said.

Ab didn't give her a break for two hours. It was clearer than yesterday, still overcast, but the clouds were higher, and it wasn't snowing. She started seeing the colors now. She felt like she was looking down into a frosted fruit bowl. Red, yellow, orange, green, brown, all tinged in white. This was his country. She could tell it. He moved with a purpose, never stumbling over the rocks like she did, even with the heavy pack on. He stopped once to point out a bull moose in the valley below, raking a massive set of dark antlers against the willows.

"Peak of the rut now," Ab said. "There'll be some cows with him. His harem."

Holly watched the big bull for minute, but didn't see another animal anywhere. She took three more steps downhill, looked back up, and there were three cows just standing there, dark and obvious with the snow on the ground. "Where'd they come from?"

"Probably just laying down, but they're like ghosts; they just materialize all of a sudden. At least it seems that way. He won't let 'em get too far away, not this time of year." After two kisses in two days, Ab was feeling a little rutty himself.

They made their first spruce grove around noon. It was dark under the spruce, nothing growing, and no snow had made it through the thick canopy. Holly had been dragging ass for the last hour, and Ab's legs were beginning to get soft. Ab took off the pack, and they both sat down against the trees.

"Well, we made treeline, and sooner than I thought. No sign of your pals so far. Let's take an hour off and eat a bite. Well, assuming we got something to eat."

"I wish you'd quit calling them that."

"Calling them what?"

"My pals. They're not my pals. I hate them. They're my enemies. You're helping me and I appreciate that, but I get the feeling you don't quite believe me."

Ab put his head in his hands and sighed. Women, fucking women. Just one word, one syllable out of place and you get the lowdown from them. Why was that? They had some kind of a microprocessor that men didn't have, always searching and sifting, looking for a raised eyebrow, a pause or a sigh out of place, and something was wrong. Bam. And it was the tone of voice. That's when you knew it. You said or did something wrong. And you were totally innocent. You didn't mean one bad thing by what you said. It just came out that way. Another guy would have blown it right off, never noticed it. But not a woman. And they wouldn't let it go. Not for a while, not 'til you "talked."

"Look, I didn't mean anything by that. Obviously, I believe you. We'll just call them the bad guys from now on. I mean, I'm bringing you with me, aren't I?" Oops, did it again.

"Well, I just wish I could make you believe me. You think there's something else going on here, I can tell. But there's not. I'm on the level. You're the suspicious type, I can tell."

That did it. It was over. He had a type. Once you've been typed, you're doomed. Women hated types. Sometimes, when he got lonely, Ab wondered why in the world he had come up here. It was coming back to him now.

"Hey, I got a can of tuna fish in here."

They were moving again in forty-five minutes. In two more hours the creek had turned north. That was good, Ab thought. They could probably be on the winter trail in one or two days at the most. Then one day to the cabin. If they didn't get shot. Ab hadn't seen anything on their backtrail and was beginning to wonder if anyone was following them at all. Then he remembered something. He stopped. "Hey, Holly, you got enough legs left to cross the creek and skirt that big mountain to the east there?"

She caught her breath and nodded yes. "But I thought you said we needed to stay north on this creek until we ran into a trail of some kind."

"Well, we do. But if I remember right from the map, there's a hot spring on the other side of that mountain. I thought we might try to find it, and we could get a bath tonight. But more importantly, if those guys, uh, the bad guys, are coming this way, they're not likely to cross the creek and start uphill. They'll want to keep going downhill and probably won't suspect we'd go back uphill either. The, uh, bad guys, that is."

"Sounds good to me." She gave him another kiss and stepped right out into the creek.

"Lord, help me," he said.

Before Ab had his boot in the shallow water good, he saw the salmon. Then another. They were spawning and darting around underfoot trying to work upstream. It took him ten minutes to toss four of them on the rocky shore. Plenty for supper. Holly had crossed the creek and just sat down and laughed at a man fishing with his bare hands. He didn't care. None of that freeze-dried crap tonight.

Ab took his knife and cut a hole in each fish jaw and put a piece of string through. He didn't gut them 'til they got around the mountain, out of sight of the creek. About twenty minutes later they heard a rifle shot, then another. "There's your. . ."—Holly darted a look at him—"the bad guys," Ab said.

"Are they shooting at us?"

"Oh hell no, they're somewhere up that drainage we were on this morning. They won't have any idea where we are. Those shots were probably two miles from here. But if they didn't leave that plane til this morning, they been picking it up and putting it down. Probably shot something to eat. That's why I don't want to shoot this .45 at game. It might give away our location. Good, good, good. Now I know where you boys are. Welcome to my world. We might just have a little hunter-huntee role reversal tomorrow."

What are you gonna do?"

"Right now? I'm going to find me a hot bath and cook some fish."

Ab found a game trail winding upward around the base of the mountain going east, and eventually hooking to the south on the backside, away from Klein Creek. The trail cut through acres and acres of lush patches of blueberries and saskatoons. He knew the area would be infested with bears, packing on fat at the rate of two or three pounds a day.

They negotiated around a huge rock and could see steam coming out of the ground.

"Found it." There were three pools, steaming and bubbling, pouring off into a small stream running to the northeast. There was another colorful valley below, sloping uphill into the biggest mountains Holly had ever seen. The ground was flat here, open and no snow at all. It was a natural camping spot, and Holly almost expected to look over and see a shiny new Toyota or Chevy sitting there. A commercial grade location. Almost as if on cue, the skies broke for the first time in two days and sunshine swept down across the mountains. "Unreal, unreal," she said.

Ab already had his pack off, picking out a tent spot. He went through the same procedure as last night, meticulous in his tent pitching. Holly sat down; her legs were whipped. She alternated her eyes from the grand landscape to the lean man setting up her bedroom, both comforting and pleasant sights. "How come there's no snow here?"

"Ground's too warm, melts it off as soon as it hits. You're sitting on top of a geothermal phenomenon." Ab stopped what he was doing for a second and took in the view. It was indeed breathtaking. He never got tired of it. Something different and interesting around every peak.

"All right, camp's set up." He took the stringer of fish and walked fifty yards north of camp to a small snow bank on a slope. He buried them there and washed his hands with snow.

"What was that for?"

"Keep 'em cold, keep the scent down. The smell of fresh salmon will pull in every bear for fifty miles."

"You think there's a bear within fifty miles of here?"

"Probably no more than a hundred of them."

"A hundred!" she screamed.

"Hey, don't yell so loud. Bears are sensitive, get offended easy. Did you notice all those berry patches we climbed through in the past hour?"

"No, I didn't notice." She was just following a backpack and watching the cute ass that was hauling it.

"City slicker." Ab shook his head. He walked over to one of the pools and checked it. It was very hot, probably too hot to stay in for more than ten or fifteen minutes. The sky was clearing up good now, just a few puffy white clouds floating by. He sat down by Holly and handed her a water bottle.

"All right, here's the deal. You just sit around here, take it easy, take a nice bath, have a shot of whiskey, whatever. Maybe a nap. We got about three hours of daylight left. I'm gonna pussyfoot back around this mountain and see if I can locate our boys. Get a fix on things. Then I can formulate a plan. Maybe we can do a little bushwhacking tomorrow instead of the other way around. If you feel like it, in a little while, you can ease down into that poplar patch and gather up some deadwood, as much as you can find. We'll have a big fire tonight. It's going to be clear and cold, but we'll be tipsy and warm. We're downwind of the bad guys and behind a mountain, so they won't see or smell anything. But be careful when you start downhill."

"Bears?" It was all she could think about. He's leaving, and there's a hundred bears out here. He said so.

"No. There's a lot of those pools down below. Some of them have what looks like solid rocks around them. But some of it won't be solid, it'll be eggshell thin. And the water in some of them is hot enough to boil your skin off. So stay away from them."

"What about the bears?" She wasn't worried about hot water. Hot water wasn't going to sneak up from behind her and rip her freaking head off.

"Aw, shit, I wish I'd never mentioned bears. They're not gonna mess with you. All they want to do is eat berries. If they were starving, that might be something else, but they're not. They won't give you a second look. They got stuff to eat everywhere they turn."

"That's what bothers me. They might look at me and see something tasty."

"No they won't. I might look at you and see something tasty, but not a bear. They're nervous of humans. They know humans can hurt them."

"I can't hurt them."

"They won't know that. If you see one, which is unlikely, just don't make eye contact, and go on about your business. They'll go away."

"If I see one, I'll be doing my business in my pants."

"Well, that'll probably make them leave too. I'll be back before dark." He started to walk off.

"Maybe I should go with you," Holly said.

Ab turned around, walked over, and put his arms around her. "You'll be fine, Holly, I promise." He put his hands on her face and held it up toward his. Those blue eyes again beaming confidence. Then he reached over, and this time, he kissed her. He turned and walked around the mountain. Wow. Then she headed straight for the Jack Daniels.

Chapter 17

ON THE TRAIL

Rusty was up at first light, cold and miserable. He wanted to start walking quick, just to warm up. Shinda and Doran were huddled up together on the floor under the blankets the woman had cut up. Shinda was snoring. Rusty kicked him. "Get up. Let's get moving. I want to catch up with those two ASAP." He especially wanted the shooter, the cocksucker who had thrown this big fucking monkey wrench in his life. Six or eight sixty-nine grainers ought to do the trick. He'd try to catch them in the open, and do it from a distance. Maybe a hundred or a hundred and fifty yards, well out of .45 range. This dude was a shooter, no doubt about it. He'd heard the shot sequence. One-two, one-two-three, fast as lightning with a ten-foot transition in between. The last shot was a head shot on a falling man. Yeah, this guy was good with a .45. Rusty had shot .45's a lot, and he knew he couldn't do that. Not with that kind of speed.

He thought they'd catch up pretty fast if they were on their trail because the woman was pretty banged up and looked pretty soft on top of that. She wouldn't move very fast. But the only way to find them was to get moving. He knew from the tracks last night they had taken off to the southeast, more confirmation that it was the way off the glacier. The guy must have heard or seen the plane go down and come up to investigate. Some kind of macho mountain man motherfucker. He'd get his soon enough, sticking his fucking nose where it didn't belong. He hoped the guy didn't have a rifle too. That would complicate things.

"Shinda, Doran. Get all the water you can carry. Let's go."

He pushed them hard all morning, but they didn't complain. They were in good shape, tough, and on more of a mission that he was. You kill a blood relative of one of these guys and you better be looking over your shoulder forever. They wouldn't let it go, didn't know how.

The two sets of tracks were faint, but they were there, all morning, all the way down. They were off the ice pack just before midday, headed down the drainage. The snow on the ground was sparse here, but they could still make out a track occasionally. When Rusty got to the rock wall, he could make out the campsite. "Son of a bitch has got a tent, a ground cloth or something."

Looking closer, he could see the holes in the ground where the pegs had been pulled up. Good, maybe he would be sleeping in a tent tonight, he thought. "Picked a good spot. No way we could have seen the tent from up top, even if we had been there. Grassy area, good windbreak, snow blew right on over it." There wasn't any on the ground by the wall. Rusty had been a good soldier before he fucked up. He was trying to learn all he could about his opponent. He got Shinda and Doran moving down the hill again. Three hours later they were approaching the treeline and could see down to the creek. They were all three tired, and they needed some food. With the brush getting higher and no snow having gotten to the ground, Rusty lost the track.

He looked over at Shinda. "Too bad we didn't get them in the open. It's gonna be tough now. High brush, trees all over, no way to track them. But I think they stayed on this drainage to the bottom down there where the creek turns north. They'll keep going downhill, and, if my guess is right, this dude's gotta have a cabin somewhere. That's where they'll be headed. We'll find it, sooner or later, if we don't find them before then. But if we don't, and this guy's got a satellite phone or a motorized way out, we're fucked. The manhunt will still be on, but it will be for us."

About a half mile from the creek, Doran grabbed Rusty by the arm and pointed. Three caribou were trotting uphill toward them, seemingly oblivious to the outside world.

"I got 'em," Rusty said. He turned the red dot sight on and got on the lead caribou. But before he could break the shot, they scattered to the wind, left and right. They weren't even looking up at the time. "Got our wind," Rusty said. Then he picked one up, angling uphill to the left, and broke off two shots before it got off into the high buckbrush.

Shinda ran up to him. "Did you get it?"

"I don't know. I felt good about the second shot, not the first." A .223 is a small caliber bullet without much weight to it. Definitely not a big game caliber, Rusty knew. He wished he had his .308 with bipods on it and a good Leupold on top. That would be the gun for out here. Maybe even something bigger than that.

"Let's give it twenty or thirty minutes, then we'll go look. I need a break anyway." Then it hit him. Shit, he might have just given their position away. It probably didn't matter. They had to eat, and she knew good and well they would be after her.

It took almost an hour to find the damn thing. It didn't go fifty yards from where he had hit it. They must have walked right by it twenty times. You wouldn't think you could lose a 200 pound animal out here, but the animal had just crumpled right down into the brush and was the same color. He felt like they were just fucking off, burning daylight. This was turning into a needle in a haystack deal, going south fast. He watched Doran slice out the backstraps and one ham with his brother's knife. He was almost as good with it too. These guys would love the meat; they would eat anything. Some of the shit they ate on the island made him sick to look at.

He needed an alternate plan. He might not find these people. He'd keep trying for a few more days anyway, but then he'd need a backup; he'd be on the lam. He knew what it would be. He would have to dump these two bozos. That wouldn't be a problem. He couldn't go walking out of the bush with two Sri Lankans trailing behind. Without Shinda and Doran, he would just turn into another tourist. He had four grand stashed on him and a passport in a different name. He would just dump the rifle after he took care of them, slip Doran's nine in his waist, and be a tourist who missed his bus. He was an American, he could blend in and pull it off. But that was the alternate plan. He wouldn't give up on the Allen woman and her pesky helpmate just yet. He would keep looking. No need to start panicking. He had food. He had time. He was special forces trained. But either way, he had made up his mind. Shinda and Doran would have to go.

"Good job, boys. Let's head for the creek."

By the time they got to the bottom where the creek turned north, it was getting late in the day. Rusty had been getting progressively worried about an ambush. He had marked their position with his gunfire earlier, and they weren't in the open anymore. It was working on him. He was studying every bush and tree now, half expecting some buckskin clad Jeremiah Johnson looking fucker to pop out and gun their asses down. He could do it, too. Double tap all three of them before Rusty could drop the star safety on his AR, and it would be the way to do it. Even if the guy did have a rifle.

He decided to make camp. It was getting late, and even though the sky had cleared off, he wanted a good lean-to and a good fire tonight in case it snowed again.

He started barking orders at Shinda and Doran about firewood and limbs for the lean-to. They were good help. He wouldn't take them out 'til he absolutely had to. "And keep your eyes peeled. That motherfucker might be around." He saw that Jeremiah Johnson image in his head again.

Chapter 18

RECON

Ab hated to leave Holly scared like that. But he needed to do this. He would hike back around the mountain, stay up high, and watch from some kind of lookout to see if he could get a fix on these guys. She needed the rest, and two people were easier to spot than one. This would be four more miles of hiking, round trip. What he mostly wanted was to get a look at this white guy, even from a distance, to see what he was up against and to verify which way they were headed. He got halfway around and then angled up off the trail they came in on, gaining elevation. In forty-five minutes he was lying behind two rocks with the Klein drainage and the corner where the creek turned north spread out below him.

He watched a bald eagle floating over the creek, looking downward and constantly turning his head, fishing for salmon. “Same menu with me tonight, buddy.” The eagle stopped in mid-air, fluttered, turned, and made a sudden dive straight down. Then, just before crashing the water, he leveled off parallel, the speed from the straight dive pushing him five yards farther along, and the yellow legs and black talons swept backwards, grabbing the heavy fish with perfect timing. Ab thought the bird would crash into the water for a second, but the wingbeats were powerful, and in a moment he had altitude again and circled a dead spruce twice before picking a limb. Ab thought about what he had seen. It reminded him of watching the great Sevigny or Leatham running through an IPSC field course, firing shots and reloading so smooth and fast that it looked surreal. Like them, the eagle had probably done it a thousand times, giving it no thought.

He could see them now, coming down in a line, the big muscular white man in the rear. He could tell by their gait that they were tired. The two men in front were both carrying things, probably meat, and maybe blankets. From a half mile it was hard to tell. As they descended and got closer, he could tell there were rifles slung over the big man’s and one of the other men’s shoulders. Two rifles to deal with and he had, what, twenty-eight rounds of .45 left. That was plenty of ammo, or should be. The problem was distance. They could get him from range, not vice versa. But first, they had to find him. They would know she wasn't alone now. This guy would, anyway. Ab had tossed the Beretta far out into the snow when he took it off the first dead man. He wouldn't carry a nine, not even as a backup. Puny piece of shit. But that hadn't fooled this big boy. He wouldn't buy for a minute that Holly had stolen the gun, killed two men, and taken off all alone.

The men reached the bottom where the creek turned, and now it was crunch time. Unless one of these guys was a Swahili tracker, they wouldn't know which way he and Holly went. The creek bed was all rocks, nothing to leave a track on. Sure enough, they turned north. Then the big man stopped them, and they started talking. There was no way Ab could hear them from 500 yards, standing on the noisy creek bank. After a minute, the big man walked up into the trees on the hillside. The two others went in different directions. Then he saw them all dragging brush and limbs up into the trees, making trips back and forth. They were making camp.

Ab belly crawled til he was around a corner, then stood up and started walking back to camp. They were safe for the night. It was his game now. What to do, what to do.

Chapter 19

NORTHERN LIGHTS

Holly had two big shots of liquid courage, got a good buzz on, and felt better about things. Ab knew what he was doing. She would be all right. Better have one more. She got up fifteen minutes later, almost fell, and staggered cautiously down to the poplar grove. There were lots of dead limbs around. Amazing, free firewood. She just kept going back and forth, piling the stuff up, until she noticed how much was stacked by the tent. About four hundred dollars worth in Beverly Hills.

So far, so good. Hadn't been chewed on yet. She decided to try out the natural hot tub. She fell down twice trying to get her pants and longjohns off. She finally decided, fuck it, and finished stripping sitting right on the ground. The water was damn hot. It took a minute or two to ease all the way down in it. The pool was about three feet deep and six feet across. If her friends could see her now. Free firewood, free hot water, and a view to knock your socks off. She was in a booze-induced euphoria now, imagining herself living out here with Ab, killing bad men, and soaking in hot tubs. She snapped out of it when she heard the little "woof." She spun around facing the tent and the trail, and there it was. A big black bear, standing on the same trail that Ab had walked off on. The instant shock wave went straight through her, the full bladder emptying involuntarily into the hot water. The bear just kept looking from the tent to the hot tub and back. "Nice bear, nice bear." Then she saw more black. Two little squirts of it on either side of the bigger bear. Cubs. They just pushed up next to her on either side, looked at Holly, and then both looked up at momma with that "what are we gonna do now" look.

Gotta quit making eye contact, Holly thought. Ab said don't make eye contact. It was hard to look away. She bit her lip and looked down at her reflection in the water. "Please God, make the bears go away," she prayed. "Please make the bears go away. Please let me live. And if I do, please give me the strength to kill that son of a bitch for leaving me alone."

She heard crashing and knew she was a dead woman. She looked up in time to see a patch of black running away from her fast. Holly sunk all the way under and didn't come up for a full minute.

* * *

Ab was figuring it out on his way back to camp. It took him a while, but then he got it. He knew exactly what he was going to do tomorrow. He stopped in one of the blueberry patches and filled his tuque up. He ate a few. They were ripe and rich in flavor. About ten minutes out from camp he saw a big black sow and two cubs running down the side of the mountain. He wondered what got them so spooked. Must have seen something big and hairy.

There was thirty minutes of daylight left when he came around the big rock into camp. He ducked just in time. The big poplar stick busted against the rock. He grabbed her arm before she could swing again. "Whoa Nellie, take it easy. Did I say something wrong again?"

Holly bent over and put her hands on her knees. "I thought you were a bear. There were three of them here just a few minutes ago."

"And?"

"And what?"

"And did they run away and not bother you like I said they would?"

"Well, they did, but that's not the point. You shouldn't leave me alone out here. It's too nerve-racking."

"So busting my head open with a stick of firewood is the answer?"

"I don't know. It crossed my mind."

"And what were we doing when this vicious bear attack occurred?"

"I was in the hot tub. And it scared me bad. You should have been here."

"In the hot tub? And did we pee in my bath water?"

"Hell no," she lied. "So what did you find out?"

Ab filled her in on the excursion and, as he was doing so, noticed the Jack Daniels bottle and the monster pile of firewood. "Good job on the firewood. We gonna stay here til spring?"

"Smart ass."

He couldn't stop laughing now. "I'll start you a fire. Then I'm gonna take a bath. After that, we'll have a nice dinner and a bottle of wine and check out the light show." He handed her the tuque. "Appetizers." Then Ab started a fire.

Holly watched as he turned his back to her, started singing an Allman Brothers tune, and took his clothes off. She eased to the side of the fire he had going to get a better look. He was well built. Strong shoulders and chest, small waist and butt. He was like a kid, sloshing around in the hot water, singing, dunking his head, and looking awfully good. The old hormones were starting to talk to her again. She had only known him two days, but it seemed like months. In L.A., you might see a guy four hours a week on a date. She'd been with Ab now for, what, twenty-eight hours. That's like seven weeks of dating in L.A. Hormone-induced justification. That's what it was. Ab just kept on singing.

* * *

Ab cooked the salmon on sticks right over the fire. Holly used the little camp stove and cooked some freeze-dried noodles. The bottle of merlot set it off. They ate off the same dish, the only one they had, the bottom of a mess kit. The salmon was what got her. She had never had it this fresh. She thought she could eat it every night of her life, and she might have to if they didn't get out of the bush.

After dinner they sat against the rocks on their pads, and every few minutes Ab would mess with the fire, adding wood and keeping it just so. Ab told Holly about the cabin, a little about the hunting operation, and how he had seen the plane go down. He told her about the Bearman and Lauren.

"But what about Ab Bailey?" How does an Alabama country boy get up here?"

He told her about how he was raised by Yul D, and later, Yul D and Aunt Ina. How they had insisted on his education. She was shocked when he told her he had a B.A. and a law degree from the University of Alabama. Then he told her about coming up with Yul D in '92 to hunt bears in Alberta with old Henry Kampet. He met Jordy, the Bearman, and they were immediate friends.

"Were you always so good at this outdoor stuff?"

"Not up here, Holly, not at first. I was pretty good back home because I was raised in a deer hunting camp. So yes, I had good outdoor skills. But this is different country. I had to learn it. I still don't know squat compared to Bearman."

"The Bearman's real name is Jordy Kampet. Outside of a few old friends from law school, he's my best friend. He and Lauren are just a different kind of people. They're like a lot of folks who live in the north country, or who live in very rural areas in the states. They prefer to live on their own terms. It's a hard life, but it's very fulfilling. People up here don't tell each other how to live, Holly. You're expected to know how to live and how to be self-sufficient."

"That's what you like about it and them, isn't it, Ab?"

"Yes, I love the freedom. And I love the challenge. Bearman will push you all the time. He's such a natural in the bush. And the man's tolerance for pain is off the charts. We were out here a few years back, bucking up fire-killed spruce for a new cabin, and Bearman cut his right thigh to the bone when his chainsaw kicked back. I was about 100 yards away. I noticed him sitting down on a log with a roll of duct tape. I didn't think much of it other than it was unusual for him to take such a long break. I didn't know he had cut himself. Anyway, he just duct taped the cut and went back to work thirty minutes later. We were back at camp before he told me what had happened. When I took that tape off, you should have seen it. The gash was full of chain oil and wood chips. I made him bite down on a rag, and I poured about a pint of Jack Daniel's into the cut to wash it out. Man, he let out a scream that would pierce your ears, then he took a swing at me. Thank God he missed. I made him drink the rest of the bottle before I would agree to sew him up. He went right back to work the next morning."

"What about Lauren?"

"She's the kindest little woman you'll ever meet, Holly. But don't let that fool you. She's little, but she's tough. And she's like a lot of women up here. There's not much she can't do. She's the best backhoe operator I've ever seen. And she bakes the best bread in a wood stove pipe that you have ever tasted. There's a lot to respect about these people. It's still a learning experience for me."

She hooked his arm in hers and pulled up close. "I think you're doing pretty good."

"Well, thank you, ma'am. Anyway, I started coming up in the spring and early fall every year between school, and helping out. Then after law school, I spent two straight years here. Then I went home for a while, got married, and well, that's another story. But hey, who wants to hear about my old dull life when I'm sitting here next to a Hollywood movie star. Tell me about your life, your movies. Have you ever been married?"

Ooh. That marriage thing. Maybe she ought to just leave out a couple of those, she thought. So she told him the Holly story. Perfectly normal childhood, beauty contests, soap opera star, TV, big screen, back to TV. Career going downhill now. That about covered it.

"How old are you?"

"I'm thirty-eight, Ab."

"I'll be damned. You're older than me."

"Great. Thank you, sir," Holly thought. She tells him about her deteriorating career, and he points out the age difference. Says it with a lilt in his voice.

"So you had a bad marriage too, huh?" Ab said.

"Well, actually, more than one."

"Ooh, two bad marriages, that's tough."

"Well, actually. . . ." She was watching him now, watching for the reaction. It was there. She could see it: from Hollywood star to Hollywood Ho, just like that. Why was three the death knell? One, no problem. Two, well it happens. But not three. It was like the mark of Cain. Especially in the real world, outside of Shakeytown.

They talked a while longer, telling each other stories of their lives, watching the stars and the northern lights. "What causes that, Ab?"

"Well, I'm not a meteorologist, but I understand it's the Earth's magnetic field, which is stronger at the poles, colliding with rays from the sun. I guess they don't get along, or they like to dance, one. It's a beautiful thing to watch though."

And it was. Holly thought it was the most beautiful thing she had ever seen. It reminded her of Casper the ghost, a cartoon she had watched as a child. "I've never seen that many stars in my life."

"No light pollution up here."

"What's that?"

"City lights at night. There's so much of it in southern California that I understand you can't pick up anything but the bright stars."

"How do you know all this stuff?"

"What can I say, I'm a smart guy. You should know that by now." He said it with a little shit-eating grin.

"A smart ass, maybe."

Ab poked at the fire.

"Was that the problem with all those husbands?"

She knew he would get back to it. Sooner or later. It was sooner than she wanted. Might as well get it over with. "No, not that. The first one, we were just young, both actors. He was a beautiful man to look at, but about as bright as my refrigerator light bulb. And he cheated, of course, because that's what men do."

"But not your dad, right?"

"No, not my dad. As far as I know." Always a zinger with this guy, and always right on the money. He was a fast thinker. And he was right: he was a smart guy.

"Well, I can see how it happens, Holly. Lots of good looking people running around, not much morality or loyalty in that part of the world. Without an awfully powerful bond, you're almost doomed from the start. But it's no reason to get cynical. To turn into a man hater. I remember several years ago we had this guy in camp. He had just gone through a bad divorce, and, man, was he pissed at women. He just kept on about it. I got tired of hearing it, so I sort of confronted him. That guy, he stuck his finger in my face and he said, 'All women are proven whores except your mother, and she's a suspect.' You sound sort of like that about men."

"Sorry. I can only go by what I've seen and experienced."

Ab poured her another glass of merlot, and then himself one. He looked at the bottle. "I wish another plane would fall out of the sky. I need to raid another liquor cabinet. What about numbers two and three? Same story?"

"Pretty much," she said.

Ab could see it in her face now. That sour look. Memory lane full of potholes. She wasn't very happy with her life, where it was going. He decided to let it go, change the subject. But she started back up, a tipsy woman, about to spill her guts.

"The second one, I caught him too, but not with a woman."

It took Ab a second to catch on: then he got it. "Oh, he had a little sugar in his tank, did he?"

She just looked at him. "Where do you come up with these phrases? Anyway, yeah, I guess he did. I mean I know he did. The third one was just stupidity on my part. I could make up a lot of other excuses, but stupid's the best one."

"Hey, don't worry about it, kiddo, I can't throw stones at you. I'm about in the same boat." He wanted to bring her mood back up, get her out of this funk. It was interesting to hear this stuff firsthand though. When he was around a TV, he had seen a few of those stupid Hollywood update shows, the ones that are always on around suppertime. They made all the stars look all happy and in love all the time, like life was some kind of utopia out there. Of course, he knew it was bullshit. He was sitting right next to the proof now. They were people without value or meaning in their lives. When everything was provided for you, you didn't have to live. That was the problem. It was why so many rich kids committed suicide. You had to work to live to want to live. You could throw any of those kids out into this environment and they would fight like hell to stay alive. It was a Zen thing. It just sounded like a stupid phrase, but it was true. Living in the present, not the past, because there really was no past or future. Ab remembered something from the Zen poet P'ang-yun when asked about life, what it was, what it all meant.

Miraculous power and marvelous activity-
Drawing water and hewing wood.

That poem just about summed it up for Ab Bailey. It was about living in the moment you were in. Bringing attention to the details of what you were doing at that moment. That's when you became a human being. Life is full when you're living it, not when you're worrying about it, he thought. He was a happy man. "Hey, Holly, what's the happiest you've ever been in your life?"

"Huh, I don't know."

"Well, think about it. When did you feel most alive? Just really glad to be here, into the moment."

She did think about it and it came to her. "Right here, right now, with you."

"But why? I mean, we're in the wilderness, might die tomorrow. You're thousands of miles away from your cushy house, your cushy life." He laughed. "It's funny, isn't it?"

"Who was this man?" she thought. She took him by the hand. "Let's go get in the tent."

She pushed Ab down onto his sleeping bag and straddled his legs. She didn't waste any time. She took off the big shirt he had given her, then pulled her undershirt over her head and unsnapped her bra. "What's this," he said. She smiled. "Appetizers." He couldn't move, mesmerized, the flickering firelight through the tent wall showing him everything. It was all roundness and smooth. Perfect. Roundness was what got a man.

You could get to him with a cartoon drawing if the roundness was there. This was real though, and it had been such a long time. Ab was growing fast.

Holly wouldn't let up. She needed this, needed it bad, and this was the man she wanted it with. It was better than she ever remembered. She stayed on top. She might kill this man. But he was definitely up to the task. He needed it as bad as she did. She could tell. And they just kept coming to her. Stored up for months. One after another. And then it was his turn. Letting it all go.

He pulled her back down and kissed her, held her. He could feel her breath, in and out, on his check. "You got thirty minutes," she said.

After the third time, Ab was starting to drift off. Just too much relaxation for one day.

"So what's this big plan you got for tomorrow?"

"You'll find out. Go to sleep." He kissed her. They both slept dreamless, people with no guilt.

Chapter 20

CONDITION RED

Rusty was nervous all evening. They got a fire going and the lean-to built, but the light from he fire bothered him. That guy out there in the bush bothered him. It would be so easy. Rusty had no night vision with the fire. The mountain man could waltz right into camp and waste them all on the spot. It wasn't bothering Shinda and Doran. They were chanting and cooking caribou. It was good, too. All he had to go with it was a bag of potato chips, which he had hurriedly stuffed in his pocket this morning.

The only other thing he had taken off the plane was a Texas mickey-sized bottle of gin. He almost busted it when he first sat down. He completely forgot it was in his back pocket all day. After three drinks he quit worrying about the ambush. Face it, they were long gone.

Headed on down the creek. The cabin, that was the key. The guy had to have a cabin. If they hadn't heard Rusty shoot, they might be feeling pretty safe by now. Maybe they would just hole up in a cabin and give her time to recoup. In a plane crash, banged up, sleeping in the cold, and walking hard all day would take its toll on her. She'd have to eat whatever crap she could scrounge. Yep, no doubt about it, whatever she was doing right now, there wouldn't be much enjoyment involved.

Shinda and Doran were at it again. Sitting cross-legged, bobbing back and forth, chanting over their dead.

"Knock it off, guys, too noisy. You want to get shot in the back of the head?"

Both men quickly got quiet and started looking all around as if they expected a full frontal assault at any second. It hit Rusty too. It was obvious. This dude had them all spooked. But unlike Rusty, fear or no fear, these guys would die before they gave it up. They didn't even want to camp, just keep going in the dark, stupidly, hell bent for leather, or revenge, rather.

"You know, boys, there's a good chance we're not going to find those two." He was looking for a response now. They both just looked up at him, incredulously.

Doran's eyes had gone crazy, and he looked like a devil through the flames of the fire. He was the worst of the two. Not as fanatic as his little brother had been, but now he had a real mission in life. It was like that with these people. On some level, they just wanted to fight. Or maybe it was just the nature of young men. Rusty was like that when he was twenty-five, just kept it hidden under a little more civilization.

"I will never give up. Never."

Shinda was shaking his head in agreement. "It must be avenged, yes."

Rusty's military ops mind was at work again. It might just work. He had to think it through. Maybe leave these two out here, alive. They'd either get it done or die. What if they just got caught? They would probably not tell about him. And so what if they did? He would be long gone. They didn't know his real name, much less the one on the passport and ID papers he was carrying. And if they didn't get the woman, she would blab anyway. Rusty just loved it when a plan came together.

All he had to do now was come up with the right ruse to get away from them. He'd give Doran his AR, take the nine, and go try to find the Alaska Highway. Then again, maybe he would keep the AR. He would sleep on it. Rusty crawled under the lean-to on a blanket. Stupid bitch had cut holes in it. It didn't matter, the fire was pushing plenty of heat under there, and it was clear out. He wouldn't get snowed on tonight. "Doran, take the first watch. Get Shinda up in three hours, then me. Keep that fire stoked." Yeah, that was it. No need to waste them. Let them go on their little revenge mission.

They would probably be dead in a week anyway. Who knows, maybe they would get lucky. As long as he came out on top, that was all that really mattered.

When Rusty woke up, it was well past daylight. He was cold. The fire was just coals. It was already sunny. It had that feel, it would probably warm up into the forties or fifties. Shinda was snoring again. There they were, huddled under a blanket again. Same shit, different day. He threw some wood on the fire and kicked Shinda. "Hell of a pair of night watchmen." He really didn't care now. He got some good sleep he needed, and nothing had happened. Yesterday's hike had been tough.

Doran got up and immediately started cooking a piece of caribou meat on a stick, chanting as he did so.

"Shut that shit up. I can't take it anymore."

"Which way do we go today?" Shinda asked.

"I'd say right on down the creek, but you boys better stay in condition red, and I mean it. Otherwise, you're little revenge surprise party might start early, with us being the ones getting the surprise. None of that sleeping on the job shit, like last night."

They moved north down the creek, Shinda in the lead, moving slow and cautious. Rusty had their attention now, and it was a good thing. This made more sense. He would stay in the rear, more time to react to an ambush, and third in line to get shot. The guy might attack from the rear, but it was more likely that they would bump into his and the woman's camp. That would also keep Rusty out of the line of fire of those two lunatics, because if they ran into that woman, they would just flat open up.

After a slow moving hour, the creek was getting bigger. It was picking up streams left and right, increasing the noise level, making Shinda and Doran edgier. Doran kept the Beretta unholstered, Shinda walking at low ready. They were loaded for bear. The willow bushes were high here, some over ten feet. There were spruce groves, poplar trees, and rocks as big as houses. Too many places to hide, too much to check out.

Rusty heard crashing noises up ahead to the left. He flinched at first, but recovered, knowing it was just an animal they spooked, probably snoozing in the sunshine. But it was too much for Shinda and Doran. They both opened fire. Shinda dumped ten rounds from the AR before Rusty could stop him, and Doran shot seven times. They were screaming and jumping up and down.

"Stop it, goddamn it." Rusty was screaming, grabbing Shinda with one hand and trying to push Doran's gun hand down with the other. Doran was going in circles, sweeping Rusty and Shinda on each pass with his finger on the trigger.

It took two minutes to get them calmed down.

Doran started yelling at Shinda now. "Did you get them, did you get them?"

"He didn't get them," Rusty said. "He might have got something, but it wasn't them." Rusty was furious.

All that noise, all of it unnecessary. Maybe he would just shoot them. Right about now wouldn't be a bad time.

"Well, let's go see what you killed." It was a juvenile black bear. It wouldn't weigh over fifty pounds. Doran already had his brother's knife out.

Chapter 21

R & R

Ab woke up first. It was a good two hours after daylight. The sun on the tent woke him. It felt like it was seventy-five degrees inside. He knew it would warm up nicely today. Like every other morning of his adult life, he woke up ready for action, the pump primed. But this time, there was something he could do about it. Besides, she owed him. He had been mighty accommodating to her last night. So he did a little poking in that direction, and she pulled him over on top of her.

"Sure, go ahead, take advantage of me."

He was kissing her on the face and noticed all the swelling was gone, just some bruises left. "If I counted right last night, you were getting about four to one on me, so let's see, you owe me nine."

"You'll never catch up." Ab kissed her afterward, rolled over, and dozed right back off.

So nice to have a man around, Holly thought. She was ready to get up. So much for this big day he had planned. She stuck her head out, did a bear check, and headed for the stove. Ab woke up again twenty minutes later smelling coffee. He crawled out, stretched, and yawned. Holly handed him a cup of coffee.

"You're turning into quite the bush woman. Where's your bear stick?"

"I'm gonna get one for you."

"Yeah, I noticed last night they do double duty."

"So I guess you scrapped those big plans you had for today."

"Nope, We're doing them. Right now."

"Doing what?"

"Taking the day off. I thought about it on the way back in last night. We both need the rest, and I don't really want to just go off willy-nilly after three guys with two AR's when all I've got is a .45. I do want to monitor them, and I do have an overall idea about what to do. But we're not going to do much today. Well, we might do a few things today." He was looking sideways at her and grinning.

"Damn you, boy, what have I unleashed here?" She looked at him, all that long brown hair, those wild eyes. A boy toy with a gun and an attitude, that's what she had.

He was rummaging through the pack now, and pulled out a package of freeze-dried grits.

"I don't know where Bearman buys all this shit. We got to scrounge up some food today. How about grits and blueberries for breakfast?"

"Sounds o.k. to me," Holly said.

"After breakfast, I got to go back around the mountain and see if they've broken camp, which I'm sure they have, and make sure they're headed north." Her eyes were getting big. "And I know, I know, you're going with me."

"You're damn right I am."

"I pretty much have to take you. I can't afford to have my head bashed in."

"It may happen yet."

Ab knew they were gone as soon as he saw their campsite. The fire was still smoldering and ravens were hopping around, fighting over meat scraps. He motioned for Holly to come over. "They're gone."

"Which way?"

"Had to be north. Everything else just goes back up into the mountains. They'll probably hit the winter trail by tomorrow. Then they'll have to decide whether to go east or west. East goes to the Canadian border. West is the trail we mostly use. They'll see the quad tracks, probably go west. In three or four miles, the quad trail goes north to the cabin, or you can stay straight to the

Chisana River, cross it, and then the trail hooks north to Jatahmund Lake, and that's the part that scares me."

"Why?"

"Because that's where Bearman and Lauren are. They might get ambushed."

"You don't think Bearman can handle them."

"Oh yeah. He's tough as hell. A lot tougher than I am, and if he sees them walking up, he'll be very suspicious. But he's the world's worst about not carrying a gun. They might get the drop on him."

"They might not do anything, you know."

"Maybe. But just the same, I'd feel better if we could get there first, or better yet, kill 'em."

They were turning to go when Ab heard the distant shots. "Stop. Listen."

There was a quick barrage of shots, some of them overlapping.

"What are they?" she asked, but Ab held his hand up and stopped her.

"Let's just listen a bit."

After a minute of silence, Ab said, "Don't know what they're up to, but it's nice of 'em to keep us posted so regular. They're headed north."

On the way back to camp, Holly couldn't even get Ab's attention. She wanted to ask him about the blueberries and the bears, find out more about the mountain ranges and the country. But she gave up. She could see it on his face. There was a lot going on behind those blue eyes.

She really didn't want to confront those three at all. She would be happy to just stay in that beautiful little campsite, eating blueberries and salmon, soaking in the hot spring, and making love. She was feeling better, her body mending. The day off was really helping her. Ab was right: if they had kept pushing, she would have just kept falling back, and they would have been overtaken. They were within two hours of getting caught yesterday. All the swelling was gone in her face and she could breathe and see out of the left side of it again. Only her stomach and legs hurt now, and most of that was not caused from the crash. All the downhill hiking had her legs sore, especially her quads, but it was a good kind of sore, and she knew those legs were tightening up in a way that no exercise machine would do. As for her stomach, it would probably already be better now, if not for all her exertion last night. "Fuck it," she thought, " It will just have to stay sore."

Holly was actually glad she didn't have a mirror to look in. A bruised up face, sloppy oversized clothes, no makeup, and God knows what her hair looked like. And she didn't care. And more importantly, she knew Ab didn't either. And how did he do it? He was out here too. But he never smelled bad or looked filthy. Just an old bear in his natural habitat, she guessed.

In L.A., if she had opened her door to a date looking like she did now, all she would have seen was the guy hauling ass, his Porsche tires squealing in her driveway. She had met a different kind of man, and she liked it.

In L.A. it was all about looks and image, and looks were king. Out here, looking at this grand landscape, it almost embarrassed her to think about all the thousands of hours she had spent in front of that big, perfectly lit mirror, primping and fretting over eye shadow and lipstick. But you had to play the game by the rules, and those were the rules in her neck of the woods.

They were back at camp around noon. Ab plopped down on the ground and put his elbows on his knees and his chin on his fists. He had so much stuff spinning through his head he couldn't sort it out. He had food problems, women problems, guys with automatic rifles problems. You name it, he had a problem with it.

Maybe he should have just tried to stay ahead of these guys, he thought. Maybe just pushed Holly hard all the way to where the quad was parked, then burned it to Jatahmund and hooked up with the Bearman. Holly could fly to Northway on the next float plane and she would be safe. She could have called home, relieved some worried minds, caught a plane to Anchorage, and then a jet for home. And they could have the law after these fuckers PDQ.

And that was another problem altogether. "God-damn you, Ab," he said to himself. "Yeah, you're a smooth, in control of your emotions, motherfucker. A sucker for a pretty, bruised face. That's what he was. Get it out of your head, man. It'll never work. If you manage to get her out of this alive, what, she's just gonna follow you around from podunk Alaska to podunk Alabama? Never happen, forget about it." He wished he had packed his copy of the *Tao Te Ching*. He needed a little propping up. He was watching her undressing by the hot spring. Just a stunning woman. None of that fake, pointy silicone shit. Boy, talk about things propping up. He decided to join her.

Ab slid down in the hot water next to Holly and smiled at her.

"He's back, " she said.

"Sorry, I've had some thinking to do."

"With that much thinking, you must have it all figured out. I mean, you did point out how smart you were last night."

"Sorry, booze makes me a little cocky."

"So what are we gonna do?" She hoped he'd say stay in that hot tub 'til spring.

"I almost wish we had just pushed on, tried to stay ahead of them. But they would have caught up. They proved that yesterday. We would probably be in a firefight right now, with the odds stacked against us. So yes, I think we did the right thing. But we gotta be smart and make good moves from now on."

"So what's the next good move?"

Ab looked back at the tent and grinned. Holly hung her head and shook it. "Come on."

Ab dozed right off again after the lovemaking. "He's an interesting man, but a typical man," Holly thought.

After a thirty minute snooze, Ab popped out of the tent. Holly was sitting on the ground, looking southeast at the huge, snow-covered mountains. The sun was shining, it was warm, and there was almost no wind. "What are those mountains, Ab?"

"You're looking at Canada, the Yukon Territory. That's the Kluane, the Saint Elias Mountains, the highest in Canada. They top out with Mount Logan. It's over 19,000 feet."

"How do you know so? Oh yeah, you're a smart guy. We already figured that out."

"You just can't educate some people," said Ab.

"I would ask you what our next move is, but I'm afraid I'd get drug back in that tent."

Ab looked down into the valley below, sunny and colorful, all the snow melted now. "I'm going down there, hunting." Holly's eyes got big again. "I guess we're going hunting," he said.

They took a game trail down into the valley, Ab looking back every few seconds, giving Holly dirty looks because of all the noise she was making.

"So what are we hunting?"

"Apparently, the dumbest animal in Alaska. They'd have to be to hang around with all the noise you're making."

"Touchy, touchy. You better be nice, mister. I might just cut you off."

"I won't have any energy for it anyway since it don't look like I'll be eating tonight."

It took about an hour and then Ab spotted the Ruffed Grouse, a covey of them, feeding along the ground. He put his hand behind him, motioning for Holly to stop.

"Chickens."

She saw them now, but they didn't look like chickens to her. She thought chickens were white, with red things on their head. She held her ground, and Ab moved up slowly. He had his gun out now, and Holly thought back to the crash. It was the first time she had let herself. God, the fear. It seemed like twenty years ago now. "Cut her throat, throw her in the crevasse. Sure, you can fuck her first, why not?" She was not in denial anymore. It didn't just happen to other people. She vowed to herself that if she made it out of this ordeal alive, she would buy a gun and learn how to use it. All her friends would laugh and look down their liberal noses at her. She had given donations to these people, money to take away all the guns. What if they had taken Ab's gun. They weren't going to use a gun on her anyway, just rape her and split her throat open. She remembered what Ab said on the first night: he didn't make the world, he just had to live in it. He didn't have a political ax to grind. He was just a free man who reserved the right to defend himself the best way he thought possible. And he had quite obviously figured out the right way. He proved that pretty quick.

She wondered how you could do that. Be so fast and so good and so smooth. Must take a lot of practice. Just owning a gun wouldn't cut it. It would take work, training. Holly wondered where would she get that. "You're staring at him, sweetheart," she thought. The guy said he was a firearms trainer.

She wanted that confidence that Ab had. The next time she walked through a dark parking lot by herself, she wasn't going to depend on hope as a strategy. Not anymore.

The shot startled her. She looked up and saw the bird, flopping around the brush, then another shot, and another bird flipping around. Ab went over and picked them both up and held them in the air. "Supper."

Ab went through the same ritual as before. He cleaned the birds, then went up on the hillside and buried them in a snowbank.

It was late afternoon now, and she was relaxed, almost dozing, on a thermarest.

Ab was rummaging through the pack again. "We got three more bags of freeze-dried and three more days worth of coffee. One bottle of wine, half a bottle of whiskey. But that's not the worse of it."

"Uh oh, what is it?"

He held up the little can. "Only one more can of dip."

"I never met anybody that put that stuff in their mouth."

"That's your misfortune, because the redneck male is the most superior specimen of the species. But I'm sure you've figured that out by now."

"Smartass."

"Just pointing out the facts, ma'am."

"Hey, Ab, you think you could teach me how to shoot a gun?"

"I can teach anything with opposable digits how to shoot a gun."

"With what?"

"You know, fingers, thumbs."

"Well, why didn't you just say that?"

"Testy, testy. I do not teach testy people how to shoot guns. Might take a shot at me when I got my back turned. Anyway, I thought you hated guns. Oh, I forgot, not my gun."

"I'm serious, Ab. I want to learn."

"O.K., it's a date. If we get out of here, we'll set it up. I'll teach you. You're having a little bit of a political shift, aren't you?"

"Well, when you've got a knife to your throat, and you're about to be raped, life takes on a different perspective."

"You've had your satori."

"My what?"

"Your awakening. It's a Zen thing. In other words, you woke up and smelled the coffee."

Who was this man? Guns and mountains and Zen stuff.

It was almost dark now, and Ab got the fire going. He had Holly cook freeze-dried chicken and rice but made her pick out all the little cubes of chicken. He had the real thing, roasting right over the fire, and didn't even want to take a bite of that processed crap. It was a good dinner, and they settled in by the fire, close together afterwards with the rest of the wine.

"So what's the plan, Ab?"

"We've got to get to Jatahmund, it's the only solution. We either go through them and kill them, or dodge them. But we got to get to Bearman. It's the only answer and that's the only way to civilization. Then we can get you on a plane home and you can get back on with your life."

She didn't like the way he said it. Just get her on a plane and get rid of her.

"Get me on a plane and get rid of me as quick as you can, huh?"

Uh oh, tone of voice. He knew he had done it again. "I didn't mean it that way," he said.

"Yeah you did. You may not realize it, but you did. You just want to be out here by yourself. That's why you're up here in the first place."

Women. A man didn't even need to think about what he was saying with a woman around. Just say anything. She'll explain it all back to you, tell you what you really meant.

"I think this conversation's a little premature, Holly. I mean, if we get killed before we get out of here, this will just be wasted talk."

"Fine, we won't talk about it. Just get me out of here and get me on a plane."

He was glad he got some loving today. It might be a long dry spell. Ab got up and got the Jack Daniel's bottle. Might as well have a drink, loosen his tongue, see what else he could fuck up.

She was mad at herself now. Been following this guy around like a puppy dog for two days, wearing her heart on her sleeve. It was the stress, the emotion of the situation. He hadn't done anything wrong. Besides, what was she gonna do. Live in a tent with this guy for the rest of her life. He was just being practical. They came from different worlds, worlds that wouldn't mesh too well. He had made peace with it, she hadn't. They'd get through this. She'd go back to her life, and he would carry on with his.

"Damn," Ab thought, "she is really getting emotional about this. Maybe there was something going on here."

The drink helped. He needed to get this relationship crap out of his head. He had a job to do here. What he said earlier was right. Nobody was going to live happily ever after if they didn't get out of here. After thirty minutes of dead silence, he decided to try again.

"Stars are something else, aren't they?"

"Yes they are, Ab."

Pretty good tone there, might try again, he thought. "So, what were you saying last night? You got a pretty big movie coming up?"

"It's not big. It's a made for TV thing. I was supposed to give them an answer by Tuesday, so I'll probably miss out on it. I wasn't so sure I was gonna take it anyway."

"I bet they'll give you an extension. Beautiful woman like you, how could they not?" Damn, that was smooth, he thought.

Holly laughed. "Beautiful women are a dime a dozen where I live, Ab."

"Well, I won't watch it if you're not in it."

She was really laughing now. "I can just see you sitting on the couch, all teary eyed watching that show. You'd be outside playing with a gun before the title got off the screen."

"Hey, I'm a new age sensitive kind of guy."

"Yeah, right." But he was sensitive, and good. A little rough around the edges, maybe. But that's what made him a man, Holly thought.

"Sometimes, Ab, I just don't know. I mean, the last few days, it's like what you said. I've sort of had an awakening. But it doesn't change anything about my life. Even if we get out of this, I'll go back to the same old thing. I rehashed my past on that wrecked plane, and it's not the pretty picture you might think it is. Maybe after all of this, if we make it out, I can change some things, correct some of what's happened to me and do a better job with my life."

"That's just dualistic thinking, Holly. All that nonsense about the past. It's not what you think it is. It's gone for one thing. The second it happened it was gone. All that remains is the spin that your brain puts on it. Learn from it, sure. Dwell on it, never. When you remember the past, your mind just picks and chooses the parts it wants to. But that's useless information. It's the whole of what happened that was, and you can never again sort all that out. And you shouldn't let it have a direct bearing on who you are at this very moment."

"That doesn't make any sense, Ab. What's happened to me is what I am. The things I did, I mean. I don't blame it on anyone but myself. I take responsibility for it. I just can't be as free-wheeling as you seem to be."

"Well, let's break it all down this way, Holly. Do you live in years, weeks, months, or days?"

"I don't know, I just live one day at a time, I suppose."

"All right, that's a start. That means you should be concerned with today, not five years ago. That's all gone. But then again, so is five minutes ago. No sense worrying about it. Just keep the good stuff. You learned some good things today. So did I. I think the problem with our brains is that they can't seem to do that simple thing. We can't just be here now; we have to throw in all this perceived past junk, and then start worrying about what hasn't even happened and what might never happen."

"That sounds fine, Ab, but how do you just shut all that stuff out? I don't get it."

"I'm not sure I do either, Holly, but I'll tell you how I go about it. First, quit quantifying things in terms of linear time. So we go from years to weeks to days to moments. But I like to break it down one more step—to get away from time altogether. My life is my breath. Instead of moments in my life, I have breaths. My breath is my life. I can go weeks without eating, days without drinking water, but no time without breath. Smokers should think about that. Wrecking their breath." Ab got up and added more wood to the fire. "Anyway, that's my time frame, if you want to call it that. Almost any problem can be overcome by concentrating on your breathing. Just think about that sometimes. Feel the air go in your mouth and your nose and then down your throat and into your lungs. Do that twenty or thirty minutes a day. It's really amazing. Eventually, you figure out that it's all you are. You are constantly breathing in and out the world of air. It's all you are, and it's all you can be, Holly."

"That sounds like some kind of relaxation technique, Ab. I don't know what it has to do with what we're talking about."

"Maybe nothing, Holly. But maybe nothing else does either. It just seems to take me out of that 'me against the world thing' and back to that 'me as a part of the world thing.' So I'm not fighting against it; I am it. Sounds weird, I know. But try it sometime."

"I'll admit, Ab, you do seem to be at peace with yourself and your life, from what I've seen."

"I try to be, Holly. But I'm not always so good at it either. I just try to be here now and stay away from being so judgmental about my life and what my brain tells me it is or has been."

"So every second, or every breath, I'm starting with a clean slate, in other words," Holly said.

"Well, not exactly. But the point is, you don't have anything but right now. This breath, at this moment, is all you have. It's what makes you perfect. Only your thoughts can make you imperfect. If you lose those, you become exactly what you are supposed to be. Get it?" Ab took Holly's cup and made her a new drink.

"Not really, Ab. I know one thing for sure, I'll never be perfect."

Ab started laughing at her. He picked up a Poplar branch from the firewood pile. "I'll give you a test, Holly. I want you to pick out the most perfectly formed leaf on this branch."

Holly studied the thirty or so odd leaves on the limb. "Well, I'd say it's either this one or this one," she said.

"Nope," Ab said. "It's a trick question. They're all perfect. They are perfectly leaves. All day, every day, they just be leaves. And it seems to be pretty simple for them to do so. So you just be perfectly you every time you take a breath. That's really all you have to do."

"I'm not sure you're all here, boy."

"I'm all here plus some. So are you. It's the 'plus some' that's the problem. Trust me on that."

"Are we gonna get through this, Ab?"

"Holly, I don't want to kid you. We've got a couple of tough days ahead of us. I'm going to push you real hard tomorrow, hard as I can. I want to get to that winter trail as soon as we can, then head west to the Snag Creek drainage. I got a four wheeler there. If we're past those guys, we're home free."

"You think we'll dodge them?"

That's the sixty-four dollar question."

"I'll be ready."

"Let's go get some sleep."

"Nope. Not until I put up some numbers. You cut it to seven today."

Ab grinned. Back in the saddle.

Chapter 22

DOWN THE CREEK

Rusty stayed pissed off for two hours. It looked like they would be eating bear meat tonight. Shinda had wasted a lot of rounds for nothing. They each just had a thirty-round mag. Forty-eight rounds left. That wasn't as bad as the Beretta though. Eight rounds left in that gun. Then it was useless. What was he thinking. It was a nine millimeter, damn near useless anyway.

The ambush thing bothered him less and less all day. Those two were running, had to be. They had passed a hundred perfect ambush sites during the day. He would have done it by now if he was going to. Rusty would just push hard, and maybe luck across the guy's cabin, and maybe not. He didn't care anymore. He just wanted to get out of this bush. He wasn't in the shape he used to be in and didn't have the right boots to be walking on these rocks and hillocks. But he kept them trudging along anyway.

The good news was that it had been downhill all the way. They hiked for ten hours with only two stops. Once at the bear, and three hours later to drink some creek water and eat the leftover caribou Doran had cooked that morning. There was a blue sky all day. Warm and clear. He wanted to get to a road or trail before the weather changed. They were grinding down fast in this nice weather, so snow or rain would just compound things. The landscape had not changed since getting off the drainage and heading north. It was mostly spruce and pine, a few poplars and willow bushes everywhere. They saw two moose and one other bear all day, all three running away when they were spotted, thank God. Neither one of those morons had opened fire again.

With about two hours daylight left, Rusty was ready to call it a day. He wanted to get his firewood up, get a lean-to built, eat some stinking bear meat and drink his gin. Besides, for the last two hours he had been falling behind. Shinda and Doran were stretched out 100 yards ahead of him. Then he noticed the hills on either side of the creek were sloping down fast. They were coming out of the big mountains now. Then he heard Doran yelling back at Shinda. A trail, he had found a trail.

Rusty caught up. Doran was down on his knees, looking for footprints. It was a four wheeler trail going east and west. It was heavy going back to the west, pretty well used. Across the creek going east, it was still there, but overgrown. The snow had melted, and there were no fresh tracks, other than a moose print.

"All right guys, let's think it through."

"They have not been here," Shinda said. "There would be tracks."

"Well they could have just stayed in the bush, but damn that would be hard walking, especially with this open trail right here. Doran, cross the creek and scout the trail going east."

"I don't think they went this way," Shinda said. "They are behind us. They have to be."

"Well, they don't have to be. They could be, but who knows. Hell, they could be anywhere. We're in this guy's backyard. Who knows what tricks he's got up his sleeve."

"I want to go back and find them, kill them. They have to pay for this," said Shinda.

Rusty thought about it. He didn't think for a minute Shinda could take this guy out, other than by dumb luck. But it was dumb luck that made him pick Shinda to go on the scouting mission at the plane instead of Amran. He might get lucky again.

Doran waded back across the creek. He was shaking his head no. "There is nothing. No tracks. That trail has not been used for a long time."

"All right, Shinda, maybe we'll try it your way. You can go back the way we came, tomorrow. Doran and

I will head west down this four wheeler trail. You can turn around when you want to, or after you kill them, whatever. You shouldn't have any problem finding us, just come back to this trail and follow our tracks. This is pretty muddy. If we get them first, we'll come back and wait here for you. I want to camp across the creek and up in the bush a ways tonight since I can't trust you guys to stand fucking night watch. Let's get across the creek and get to it, then cook that fucking bear meat."

He would be rid of Shinda tomorrow. Probably keep Doran on for a couple of days. He'd keep playing it by ear. They had a trail now. They might get lucky in a day or two and come across somebody on a four wheeler. If he heard one coming, he would step off the trail, hide, and then kill them and go. If they came up on a cabin with people, he would kill them and take their transportation. That simple. He was feeling better. He agreed with Shinda. They were in front of them now, which meant the authorities probably didn't know anything. Just a couple more days and maybe he would be out of this jam.

Rusty stretched out on a blanket while the other two tended to the fire and cooked. His feet were hurting him. He had no good food, not enough clothes if the weather turned bad again, and the odds were stacked against him. It actually felt pretty good. He liked a challenge, and not just a hard football game physical one. He liked a life or death struggle. These boys liked it too, on some level. Everybody needed confrontation. Some folks just needed more significant confrontation than others. If people didn't have it, they created it. The war he had fought in, and the other confrontations, were all fought over fabricated excuses. It was usually for land or wealth, and lately for petroleum. And you could always throw in religion if you didn't have anything else to fight over. Rusty thought the western world had gotten a pretty good handle on not starting wars over religion, but those Middle Eastern folks seemed to make a habit of it. All religions had "Thou shall not kill" high on their list of no-no's, but they could all justify a lot of killing.

You could make all the excuses you wanted to, Rusty thought. And there would always be one that satisfied the killer at the end of the day. "You took my land," or "you want my oil," or "you touched my wife." There was never a shortage of excuses for taking a life. The best one was, of course, "you pray to a different invisible man than I do, so I've got to kill you." Thou shall not kill, my ass, Rusty thought.

Rusty had made peace with taking life a long time ago. Besides, it was what he had spent his entire adult life learning how to do. As a young untested soldier with three years of training, you want nothing more than to be in a good fight. Then, about three minutes after you are in your first one, you want nothing more than to be out of it. The magnanimous part of battle was not the killing of others, but the putting of ones own life on the line, willing to chance the sacrifice of everything for what you believed in.

Rusty's belief system had changed. He still wasn't bothered by the killing part, but now he believed in Rusty. After all he had seen and been through, he understood the correct way of living a twenty-first-century life. The best part for Rusty was that he had developed the skills to back it up. Unlike the cocky cocksuckers he saw running their mouths on TV, Rusty had the skill at arms to back it all up. It was very politically correct to put it all down these days, to hate a man who was really a man—but that was all a lie, Rusty knew. He saw it in L.A. and especially in San Francisco. Utter hatred for men like him. But that was only a pretense. The same people made the movies. Not the sissy films that did o.k., but the blockbusters like the James Bond movies and the action movies, always featuring a John Rambo, a man like Rusty. And that's where people gave away their true beliefs. They flocked to those movies because secretly, deep down, they all wanted to have the moxie of a man like Rusty. In reality, they admired him. Only on the surface did they hate him. But Rusty had his answer for the world and all its condescending, hypocritical bastards. It was a phrase on a t-shirt he had bought in New Orleans in one of those tourist stands on Bourbon Street. He was drunk at the time and thought it was funny. Now he believed in it with all his heart. "Fuck you you fucking fuck."

That slogan captured the correct attitude. The one that was going to get him out of this mess. He would love to settle the score with the mountain man, but right now it was all about Rusty. Get out of it and go away. So the challenge of it all didn't bother him. It was just another test of his skills. It would be the after-action effects that would get him, Rusty knew. Nobody to share it with, no one to go home to. You couldn't tell it all to the sympathetic ear of a Sri Lankan whore. That, unfortunately, was Rusty's end game. Nobody to share his life with. But he could shake that off too with enough gin and time. Doran called that supper was ready.

The bear meat sucked. He would kill a caribou tomorrow if they came across one. Rusty slept well under the circumstances, tired from two days on foot. It was warmer than the night before. About two hours before daylight he heard Shinda leave camp, a man on a mission.

Chapter 23

MAD RAVENS

It was another bluebird day, and Ab thought it would be warmer than yesterday.

He had Holly up at first light. They had coffee and leftover grouse, then he packed camp while she washed the dishes. In another thirty minutes he had it all packed.

Ab didn't have much to say this morning, and Holly didn't bother him. The man could just change gears on a dime. Yesterday he was playful, goofing off, just wanted to snooze and make love. Today, she didn't even want to make eye contact with him. The intensity and the wildness was back, a scary looking man, if you weren't on his side. It was the man at the plane, with the potential for extreme violence, a man you didn't want to cross or provoke.

Ab faced Holly and said in a slow, measured voice, "Holly, try hard to keep up. Let me know if I'm going too fast for you. We really need to go until we get to the creek. We'll stop there and check it all out good. Then we're going to move fast but cautious. I just know they will be to the winter trail today. I don't know what they'll do then. Probably follow it west, but when they don't see tracks in that trail, they will probably guess we're not in front of them. Depending on how bad they want to kill you, they could turn back and try to ambush us. It's just a chance we'll have to take. Then again, maybe they want to get out of here as bad as we do."

She was getting scared again. Talking about men wanting to kill her drove home the reality of the situation.

"I'll do my best."

"We're gonna be fine, Holly." Then he smiled, gave her a kiss, turned and started walking. Holly looked back at the little campsite, the grass bent down in the rectangle where the tent had been, the valley below and the huge mountains beyond, with the morning sun bringing it all to life. Then she felt a little sad.

She had trouble keeping up all morning. His pack was lighter now and he was pushing hard. The day off was the key, getting the sleep and rest she needed. He knew that too. Without the time off, she would have been dead by now. He could have stayed ahead of them on his own, but, without the rest break, she could not have done it. It was tough enough to follow this man on fresh legs.

Ab stopped in the middle of the blueberry patch and waited for her to catch up. He was staring down the side of the mountain when she got to him. Ab pointed down the side of the hill. "Friends of yours?"

Holly looked down and saw them. Three black bears, a sow with two cubs, a hundred yards away, all three standing up watching the two of them. Funny, she didn't feel scared now.

"Didn't pee in my bath water, bullshit," he said, starting to walk again.

They crossed the creek thirty minutes later. Ab rummaged around Rusty's campsite a few minutes. "Built a nice lean-to. The guy's got some outdoor skills. Let's get moving, keep your eyes peeled."

It was nerve wracking walking down the creek. It was thick on both sides, high willows and dark stands of spruce. A bad area to bump into a grizzly bear or a man with a pig nose and a rifle. Holly didn't want to see either one. But somewhere down inside, she was playing out a fantasy. She kept seeing Ab gun the man down, watching him fall, suffering and in pain, paying for what he did to her. Too bad that mushy Matra Langdor wasn't stuck out here with them. Guys like that always got away, hiring other people to do their dirty work for them.

Walking and looking at Ab, Holly wondered how she had ever gotten mixed up with a man like Matra Langdor. If Ab Bailey had been the secret admirer who showed up at that party, she would have avoided him like a grizzly bear. His looks would have appealed to her, but only on an animal level, never on an equal social footing. No, she would have picked Langdor over Ab back then and made the same stupid mistake she had really made. But Holly knew she was imagining a situation that could not have been. Ab Bailey would never have lowered himself to even set foot in a room with the likes of the people she cavorted with. Walking along behind Ab, Holly wondered what this man really thought of her. In her other life, which is how she thought of it now, she wouldn't have given Ab the time of day. Maybe sign an autograph and smile, then quickly be on her way. So what did he think? Reversing the situation, the way it was, they had met in his Hollywood, the mountains of Alaska. Maybe she should ask for his autograph.

"Hey, Ab, if we had met in Hollywood, would you have asked for my autograph?"

"No," was all he said without looking back, and kept on walking.

"Thanks for your support."

She knew why. He didn't look up to other people. He wouldn't fawn over an idiotic actress like her. He didn't make love to her like a man in awe either, the way other men had. He made love to her like a man. It was his philosophy of life, and she was beginning to understand it. No one was above him, but no one was below him either. She came into his life, and he didn't question it or assign some mystical reasons to the gods above. Holly Allen was just Ab Bailey's ward in the bush and he would do his best to keep them both alive. Where he would let it go beyond that, she had no idea.

In two hours, Ab called a break. "How you holding up, kid?"

"I'm all right. How much walking we got to do?"

"I'd say maybe ten more miles to the trail. Then let's see, three miles to the cutoff to Carden Lake, then maybe four or five to the four wheeler. Could be six."

"About twenty miles then?"

"Think you can stay up with me, do it in two days?"

"I can do it in one if you say we got to."

"You could, could you? I must have pumped too many of them Ab vitamins in you."

Holly threw her head back and shook it. "Lord, give me the strength, not for the walk, just to put up with this man for another day," she said for Ab's benefit. Then she noticed all the ravens overhead. She pointed up. "What's that all about?"

Ab turned and looked. "Something dead down the creek. Maybe those guys shot each other yesterday, went ahead and committed suicide, knowing what they were up against."

Holly's mouth dropped open for a second, it never having crossed her mind that these guys might have been shooting at each other yesterday.

"Just kidding, Holly."

They got down to where the ravens were, and the birds immediately disbanded and landed in the spruce trees. They were heavy birds, bending down the spruce limbs, squawking and cawing with a piercing noise that rolled up and down the creek bank, obviously pissed about the intrusion.

"Gotta be something dead over in the willows here." The piece of brass caught his eye. He picked it up and studied it. "Two two three. This is where they were when we heard the shooting yesterday." He handed Holly the piece of brass. "I'm gonna go in the bushes here and see if I can figure out what they shot. Look around on the ground for more brass. Especially brass that looks different than this. See what else they're toting, maybe." It took Ab two minutes to find the thing, a little year and a half old black bear cub. They had cut the little backstraps out and the hams off the back.

Holly was bent over, looking. She found two more pieces of brass, both identical to the one Ab had handed her. Then she saw a smaller, shorter looking piece. She reached down, picked it up, and was just about to yell at Ab when she saw him. One of the men from the plane, coming around a bend in the creek, a rifle in his hand, like the one Rusty had. The shock wave of fear hit her, and she was frozen for a second, unable to move. He was looking up in the spruce trees at the screaming ravens, and then he looked down and saw her. He started raising the gun, smiling the same smile that Amran had when he called her out of the plane. She involuntarily screamed "Ab" at the top of her lungs, and lunged for the willows he was in.

Shinda was a maniac now, dropping the safety and pulling the trigger as fast as he could, not bothering to use the sights at all. He had her now, the filthy bitch. He would cut her in two with the rifle, find her dead body, cut her throat, cut her to pieces. He was tearing up the willows now. He could see the limbs splattering, flying up into the air, and she was in there, dying.

Holly hit the ground hard, pieces of the willow bushes splattering all around her, but she fell in a small depression, protecting her from the rounds. She covered her head, and screamed for Ab again.

Ab flattened out as soon as he heard the semi-automatic open up. He knew immediately that the man was firing wildly, too fast. Limbs were popping off up in the willows, then low then high again. The man was just firing hopers. Spraying and praying. Ab was screaming over the gunfire. "Stay low, Holly."

After about fifteen rounds, the firing stopped. Ab looked around. He grabbed the back leg of the bear and crawled, as low as he could, up to Holly. He put his left index finger to his lips and gave her the be quiet sign.

She saw the .45 in his right hand, a bear leg under his arm. He inched his way to the edge of the willows. He could make out the man's legs, moving forward slowly. Ab got up slowly on his knees, crossed his left arm over his body, and leaned right. He got a good grip on the bear leg with his left hand. Then he slung it, right out toward the man.

Shinda saw the movement, reacted, fired four rounds at the object coming toward him, then felt bullets hitting him in the chest, staggered, and fell to the ground.

Ab just let himself fall on over as he threw the leg, firing two rounds strong hand before he hit the ground and got his left hand on the gun. The man was staggering and Ab fired three more times, following him to the ground.

Holly was watching it all, more scared for Ab than she had been for herself. Same story, different chapter. Ab was too fast for the man, and he was accurate. She heard the man gurgling, a sickening sound, as if he were trying to breathe water. Holly got it now: the man was drowning in his own blood, five shots through the lungs. After a minute he was quiet, not moving. She was watching Ab's reaction. It was the same as at the plane. He waited, just stayed there with his gun out, not in a hurry to put it away. Then he reached back with his left hand, got a fresh magazine, brought it alongside the gun, and exchanged it with the one in the gun. She understood it. He was getting the gun loaded back to capacity, and doing it in such a way that he never even had to look at it. He kept the gun pointed where he wanted it during the whole maneuver.

He finally took his eyes off the man and glanced back at Holly. He gave her the be quiet sign again. He didn't move a muscle for ten more minutes.

Ab was sure the other two had to be around. He just lay there, senses wide open, a man in full combat mode. Why would they do it this way, one guy attacking at a time, and why start the ambush when he was behind cover. Maybe this guy just broke cover, screwed up the plan. If so, the other two would be out there, waiting for him to make a move, relax, expose himself.

When Ab had slung the bear leg, he only let his head and arms be exposed from the willow bush as he fell over. The man with the rifle just couldn't pick it up that fast, and Ab knew it would happen the way it did, as long as he concentrated on getting his hits. Yul D's training was paying off. They had simulated these situations in classes for years. Ab was always the assistant, when he got old enough, and Yul D barked orders at men who paid him good money to learn defensive pistol skills. "All right men. Now we can't walk the streets making the first move on people because we don't like their looks. And that's the problem. We have to give the bad guy the first move because we don't know who's bad and who's not. And I suppose it's the courteous thing to do." His students usually laughed. "But if he's got us in a duress situation, we can now turn the tables because we have the element of surprise. A distraction is best. People will always look at fast, unexpected movement. It's involuntary, they can't stop it, and it buys you the time to get your weapon in action and get the first good hits. Just make sure they're good hits."

Ab had performed a textbook distraction move. But he didn't want to do that again. He wanted to be the guy who made the first move next time instead of having to react and improvise like he had here.

Holly lay there, wondering what Ab was up to. He just kept lying there, watching, listening. After what seemed like an eternity, he slithered back over to her, but still wouldn't let her talk. They crawled thirty yards out of the willows and into a stand of young spruce away from the creek. They were totally hidden. He looked over at her and whispered, "Three down, two to go."

"Are they out there? Did you see them?"

Ab shook his head no and continued to stare toward the creek, still lying on his stomach, the .45 in his hand.

He waited thirty more minutes but didn't see or hear anything else. He knew if the big man was out there, he would have tried a flanking move by now. Ab decided he wanted to crawl back up and get the AR off the man he had killed. He owned four of them himself and knew them inside out. Then he would really have the odds evened, one rifle to one. He looked at Holly.

"Stay put for now." He slithered back through the willow patch, up to the edge by the dead man. A red delta of blood was seeping and winding through the rocks of the creek bank, going downhill. Ab was working the rifle sling over the man's head when he noticed the gun's bolt locked open. Damn it all to hell, the rifle was empty. Shot his last rounds at a bear leg, same damn bear he shot his first rounds at yesterday. Some irony there somewhere, Ab thought. He went through the man's pockets, looking for another mag or loose rounds. Nothing.

Ab crawled out on the creek bank and took a long look around. If they were out there, going to open up on him, they would do it now. Nothing but pissed off ravens. He looked up at them in the spruce, afraid to fly back down to the bear, screaming their heads off. "What are you mad at me for; I'm the one providing fresh meat."

He relaxed a bit now. The man had to be alone. Came back on some kind of assassination mission. "Holly, I think you can come out now."

She walked out of the willows and looked down at the dead man. "God, the blood. You just don't realize how much blood is in a person."

"You ought to rip open a bull moose sometime."

"Well, at least we got a rifle now."

Ab handed it to her. "Here. You can hit me over the head with it next time I say something wrong."

The joke was lost on Holly. "Don't you think you ought to carry this thing?"

It's empty, Holly, useless." She could tell he was disgusted.

"Won't your bullets work in it?"

Ab hung his head and rubbed his face with his hands. "You definitely need a gun class."

He shouldered his pack and took a last look at the man, there in his final resting place, a few minutes away from having his eyes pecked out by ravens. Then he looked at Holly.

"Looks like I shot an unarmed man."

Holly held out the rifle. "What about this?"

"Toss it. Let's make some miles."

Chapter 24

THE CABIN

Rusty woke up when he heard Doran starting the chanting ritual again. Shinda was long gone. Rusty had a headache; he was dehydrated. He looked over at the gin bottle, empty. Doran was cooking bear meat again, but Rusty knew he couldn't eat any more of it. He just wanted out of here. He wanted a good meal, a hot bath, and a comfortable seat on a bus headed to the nearest airport. It was going to be another nice day, and he wanted to make the most of it.

"Let's get a move on, Doran. Stay alert. Especially your ears. If we hear a four wheeler coming, get in the bush and hide. I'll shoot them off the thing and we'll take the ride."

If that happened he might kill Doran too, on the spot. He didn't know; he'd play it by ear. A good soldier improvises, makes on-the-spot executive decisions. That, more than anything, kept a man alive in hostile environments. You had to be willing to do the hard thing anywhere, anytime. Nobody was better at that than him. He could kill anybody, anywhere, any time, and just walk away. Sleep like a baby at night.

The trail was easy walking. It was muddy from the snow melt, but it beat the rocks and willow patches of the creek. They moved fast, always watching for tracks. A lot of game had used the trail, but no human footprints. Rusty recognized the bear and moose tracks, but not all the other smaller prints. In less than two hours, he saw the fork.

They had a decision to make. Both trails were well used, one going north, the other continuing west, the way they had been going. Rusty studied the terrain. The trail that headed north went out through the low hills away from the mountains. The trail to the west skirted underneath the mountains, sort of a north border to them. He had his bearings now, and knew basically where he was in relation to the plane crash. He looked up at the top of the mountains. This is where they came over, saw the low hills to the north, and turned the plane back to the glacier, he thought.

He knew north would be the way to go. West would take him away from the Alaska Highway, or from a road that would get him to it. Damn, he wished he had a map. But it was decision time, and he was going north.

"Doran, we'll go north. Shinda will see our tracks, know which way we went." That might be a problem too, he thought. He'd deal with it when it happened. At least he was out of the big mountains.

Doran got out ahead of him again, the younger man able to move faster. Rusty was wearing down fast. The wrong clothes, shoes, hard walking and bad food were taking their toll.

He had been living too soft for too many years now. He was still strong as a bull, but he had a gut now and his cardiovascular wasn't what it used to be. It pissed him off watching the younger man moving so effortlessly, having to stop and wait on him every few minutes. "Ten years ago I would have walked you in the ground, you little shit," he thought.

He was just trudging now, watching Doran gradually increase the distance from him. He saw a corner of a lake coming up on his right, obviously a very big lake. When he looked at Doran again, he saw the man crouched down in the bushes, motioning to him. Rusty got down low, duck walking forward. Maybe they had lucked up and found the woman.

Rusty came up alongside Doran, looking ahead. "Cabin," Doran said. Sure enough, there it was. Perched up on a steppe, a level area, was a small log cabin with a red tin roof. There were two outbuildings and no smoke coming from the chimney. After five minutes, they had seen no human activity.

"No one is there," Doran said.

"Don't be so sure. The motherfucker might be laying over in the bushes waiting on us to just saunter right up. He'll have long guns here, for sure. But this is his place. I know it. I can feel it. Let's just wait a while, recon the place. We ain't in that big a hurry."

Thirty minutes later he was getting convinced. The guy wouldn't do that. Just lie out in the weeds all day on the off chance that he would find the place. And how did he get here if he did; they hadn't seen one human footprint all day.

"All right, Doran, let's go up there, easy. Get that pistol out, be ready."

They worked their way uphill, but it was obvious they were alone. Rusty had Doran swing open the door while he covered. He went in cautiously, looked around. "Nobody home." He checked out the entire place. Bunks, clothes, guns, canned goods, even a bottle of whiskey. He had hit the jackpot. He could rest up, have a decent meal, retool. He sent Doran to check out the outbuildings and look for a four wheeler, a speedy way to get out of here. Doran came back with a caribou backstrap, grinning.

"What else did you find? What about a four wheeler?"

"No. And no more trails. The trail in here is the only one."

That was not good. They would have to hike the three miles back out and go west on the other trail. But this side trip would be worth it. They had food, guns, and shelter, and Rusty was damn tired. He told Doran to get a fire going and cook the caribou meat. Then he went outside to check things out for himself. He was looking straight back up into those big mountains. He could make out the edge of the big glacier. Four or five miles west and south, atop a very high drainage.

He knew that was where they landed the plane. He thought it through. The guy was right here. He saw it all. But how did he get up there so fast. He couldn't have climbed up that wall. No fucking way. If he had those kinds of balls, Rusty didn't want to run into that cocksucker. Ever.

Chapter 25

INTO THE DARK

Holly stayed on edge all afternoon. The killing got to her. Ab just kept her plodding along. She could see it in him too. His head was constantly moving, checking out every rock, bush and tree. It was stressful, and walking down the creek bank was not easy. She never seemed to hit a flat spot, and the boots were too loose on her feet. Ab had made her change bandages daily, but, with the uneven terrain, they would pull away from the blisters and then float around in her socks, irritating her.

He gave her a break every two hours, but by late afternoon she was dragging.

"Take another fifteen," Ab said. "How are you doing?"

"If I had decent shoes, I'd be O.K. These are too big and this ground is so damn uneven.

"What happened to the shoes you had on the plane?"

"One of them got broken in the crash."

"Were they pretty good hiking boots?" He grinned at her.

"Not bad if you were hiking through Macy's. How much farther are we going this evening?"

"As far as I can get you to go, right up to dark if you can. It'll be Spartan tonight, love."

"He called me love. He called me love," Holly thought. She could walk to the North Pole now.

An hour before dark Ab called for another break. He could see that Holly was struggling. Her gait was strained, and he knew her feet were not holding up well. He sat her down next to a boulder on the creek with willow bushes on either side.

"I want to wash your feet and change those bandages, Holly. We still have a long way to go. I need you to hold out as long as you can." Ab went through the ritual again, washing Holly's feet in the creek and drying them with his shirt. We're about out of bandages," he said.

Holly was looking at the blisters on her heels and the balls of her feet. "Those are some pretty ugly feet, aren't they?"

"Oh, I don't know," Ab said. "I've seen worse looking dogs than these." He finished changing the bandages, then kissed her on the big toe and smiled at her. "Does that make them better?"

"Anywhere you kiss me makes me better."

"I'll try to remember that, especially around bedtime," he said. Ab went to the creek and filled up a nalgene bottle with water. He handed it to Holly.

"I thought you weren't supposed to drink water straight out of a stream, Ab. We seem to do it all the time."

"I always do it up here, Holly. Back home, that's true. It's called Giardia, and it'll make you sick as hell. If you drank stream water around L.A., you'd probably grow some new green appendages. I guess a guy should filter his water, or boil it, before he drinks it. But I've been drinking unfiltered water up here for years without getting sick. Besides, we got no filter, and I'm too lazy to make a fire or crank up that stove every time I want a drink of water."

Holly was listening to Ab go on about the water and looking at the flowing creek running north, just gurgling along on a beautiful Fall day. Then she spotted the big bear headed toward them on the other side of the creek. She grabbed Ab by the arm and pointed.

"Well, looky, looky," Ab whispered. "Mr. Griz is coming for a visit."

"Don't you think you better shoot him, Ab?"

Ab looked at Holly and laughed. "With a .45? Why in the world would I want to do that? If he even felt it, it would be a miracle. Besides, if he did, he might get pissed off, come over here, and shove it up my ass. And he might not kiss on you like I do." Ab looked at the big grizzly, who had no idea they were across the creek. The bear was a carbon copy of the one who had showed up at the caribou kill, or maybe the same one. They could cover tremendous distances when they were feeding, Ab knew. The bear was just walking along, carefree, looking for something to eat. Ab leaned over to Holly and whispered, "I bet he'll top 700 pounds."

"I think you need to shoot him," Holly said. "He looks too scary. If he sees us, we're doomed. Won't your .45 kill him?"

"Yeah, and so will a croquet mallet if you sneak up on him and hit him in the right place. But it's not the weapon of choice. Besides, he's not interested in us. Bears have poor eyes. He don't even know we're here. But he will in about ten seconds. Then watch what he does."

Holly didn't have to watch. She knew he would come splashing across the creek and eat them both. He had that look.

Ab could feel the low breeze angling southeast across the creek and knew the bear would get their scent any second. The big silvertip stopped suddenly, stood on his hind legs, and started working his nose. He looked straight across the creek at the big rock. Holly knew the beady little eyes were boring a hole straight through her and that the bear could sense her fear. He would come straight for her, she knew. He would rip her to shreds, chew her up, then probably wink at Ab and go on his way. But he didn't. He turned slowly away from them, still standing, then blasted into the bush like he was being chased by a pack of hounds. Holly breathed for the first time since she had spotted the bear. "Why would he run away from us, Ab?"

"Because he has a pretty good understanding of how the food chain works. And he ain't on top anymore. Five hundred years ago, one of his ancestors would probably have come on over and had supper. But not now. Not since the old smokepole came into vogue. It's like I told you. Bears know that people can hurt them. And they hate pain. He's probably twenty or twenty-five years old. I'm sure he's had some lead lobbed at him from time to time. He's a pretty nice trophy. So he associates pain and loud noises with that smell, neither of which he cares for. Now, if we had some good smelling food over here, which we don't, he might have tried to challenge us for it. As it was, he didn't need the hassles, so he decided to leave. The bigger and older the bear, the less likely you are to have trouble with him. But they are to be respected at all times."

"Could we outrun him, Ab?"

"Hell, no. That bear could outrun a quarter horse for a little ways. They're sneaky fast. That bear you just saw can break the neck of a bull moose with a single blow. They have incredible power."

"They're that strong?"

"Oh, yeah. A 100 pound bear could kill the biggest NFL lineman alive in about five seconds."

"What about that cub they shot? Could he kill you?"

"Probably not. But he'd be like fighting the worst dog you ever met. Just don't let one get too close to you, that's all."

"How do they smell things so good, Ab?"

"I don't know, Holly, but I'd give anything to have that sense of smell. It's part of that breathing thing I was talking about. I think it's why animals have a better understanding of the world than we do. They trust their eyes and their ears, but they verify through their nose. I mean, we just have no comprehension of how good a bear or a deer or a dog's nose is. We know they can smell things thousands of times better than us, but it's all the other information they get from smell that we don't. They can sense fear or sex or weather, and who knows that else. There is an entire world of odor out there that we're not privy to because our little puny noses suck so bad." Ab was lacing up Holly's boots as he talked.

"We developed this allegedly superior brain to compensate for our lack of smelling ability. So we're so proud of ourselves for our brain. Of course, every day our superior brain gets better and better at figuring out how to annihilate the entire planet. I mean that is the end game, isn't it?"

"What about all the medical advances and stuff, Ab? We live a lot better than the animals, don't we?" Holly leaned over and lay on Ab's chest.

"I don't think so, Holly. It's taken us two thousand years to increase our life expectancy from thirty-five to seventy-five. A Galapagos turtle lives to be two or three hundred years old. Redwood trees live for thousands. All without our brain. And Galapagos turtles don't use that three hundred years scheming up ways to make nuclear weapons. If you could talk to a dog, he would laugh his head off at you. All that DNA crime technology would just be a waste of time to him. If humans had a dog's nose, we would just saunter down to the crime scene, take a whiff, then go smell the suspects and put the guilty party in jail. I suspect O. J. Simpson would be behind bars now.

"And marital infidelity would be way down, too. You cheat, you come home, the old lady smells it on you, and wham, you lose all your stuff. I think it's why dogs are not monogamous and why they call their females bitches. You see, the male dogs kept smelling other male dogs on their females, so they just gave up. The stinking bitch is going to cheat anyway, so why bother." Ab was laughing now at his own analysis of a dog's life.

Holly was shaking her head. "The world accord to Ab. The guru of the understanding of life. I think I'd rather walk on blistered feet than have to listen to anymore of this."

"Fair enough. Let's get moving."

He went past dark. She wanted to stop him, but didn't dare. It was safer moving after dark, she knew. They were moving quietly, with the creek noise covering for them. There was no way to get lost, just follow the creek downhill. Ab kept looking up high on both sides of the creek. She kept her pace right with him in the dark, stepping on his heels occasionally. She would have glued herself to his backpack if she had had some Elmer's. She stepped on his heel again. Ab stopped and turned around, obviously getting a little irritated.

"Am I going too slow for you?"

"Uh, no, I'm just trying to be a good soldier, you know, keep pace."

"Well, why don't you keep that pace about ten feet back."

Ten feet. Like hell she would. If she was going to bump into something out here in the dark, it was going to be him, not a fucking bear. "How much farther tonight?"

Ab looked up at the hills and blew air out of his mouth. "Not much. I've just been watching the hills taper off, and I think we're close to the trail. We've either walked a lot farther today than I thought, or it wasn't as far as I thought. I've never been this way, just seen it on the map. If you're up to it, I think we can get there in less than an hour."

"I'm up to it."

"Then let's hit it."

Ab took one step and she stepped on his heel again. He turned around and shoo'd her back a step. "Damn you, woman."

They cut the trail thirty minutes later. Ab got down on a knee and looked in the mud. "Yep. They're headed west now, both of them. Let's pull back in the trees here and I'll get camp up. No fire tonight."

Holly was tired. Her feet were killing her, her legs exhausted. She crawled right in the tent as soon as he set it up.

Ab boiled some water and cooked freeze-dried chili. He took it in the tent. Holly was already in her sleeping bag, exhausted. "It's not very good, but eat some anyway." She ate the chili without much of an appetite, watching Ab as she did. He was working it over in his mind again, figuring out what to do.

"You know what we're gonna do tomorrow, Ab?"

"I do, depending."

"Depending on what?"

"On whether their tracks cut off to the cabin or go on west. Could be both."

"How's that?"

"Well, one of them could go one way, and one the other. Or they could have gone to the cabin, ransacked it, and come back to the trail. We might bump into them coming back this way. I don't know."

Bumping into them; that's the part that got her. She could see the man, the one today, standing there with the gun. If it hadn't been for those birds. They might not get that lucky tomorrow. "So we're just gonna walk right down that trail tomorrow?"

"Yeah, but we're gonna do it before daylight. I want to be to the cutoff to the cabin before it gets light. Think you can do it?"

"If you say do it, I'll do it. But what if they're camped right on the trail, and we bump into them in the dark?"

"If we're being quiet, and you're not stepping all over me, they probably won't hear us. But if you hear somebody, just run like hell into the bush. They can't shoot you if they can't see you."

"When are we leaving?"

"Four or five hours. I'll get you up. We better knock off the extracurricular tonight."

"Don't matter. I'm so far ahead now," she said.

"You're proud of that, aren't you?"

Holly hugged him tight and fell asleep fast.

Chapter 26

RETOOLED

Rusty felt better after a good meal. He had caribou, a can of beans, and corn. He took the Jack Daniels bottle and stretched out on the bunk, tired and sore, but getting relaxed. Doran was studying the assortment of firearms on the top bunk. There were three scoped rifles, two shotguns, and four handguns. One of the shotguns had a shoulder stock, the other a pistol grip. Both were twelve gauge pumps. Doran liked the shotguns. He had never shot a scoped rifle. He picked one up and tried to look through the scope but couldn't get the eye relief right. He kept trying to hold his eye right up to it so that all he saw was a small image with a halo of black circling around it.

"Hold your eye further away from it," Rusty said. But Doran couldn't get the hang of it.

"Roll it down to a lower power," Rusty said. But Doran didn't know how to do that either.

"Just stick with the pump shotgun. I know you know how to use that." Doran agreed. He found a box of buckshot and started stuffing the pistol grip shotgun full. Then he would rack one in the chamber, rack it out, and feed another one into the bottom. After the fourth time, Rusty had had enough. "Go fuck with that thing outside; keep an eye out."

It was almost dark now, and Rusty was going to sleep in a warm bed tonight. He would get a good night's sleep and head out sometime tomorrow. There was an extra backpack here and he would have it full of food for the trip out. He would have warm clothes and a sleeping bag and tent. He was set. He would take the mountain man's short 308 and plenty of ammo. The hell with that AR. Things were looking up, as long as the guy didn't pop in tonight. And if Rusty came across them tomorrow, he would just loop up and blow their goddamn heads off with a real bullet. He would give the Allen woman some love, 168 grains of it.

Doran came back in at dark. He had already changed his wardrobe to clothes from the cabin. This guy's clothes fit him well. Doran was restless. Rusty could tell. If he ever got up close to the Allen woman with that pump, it would be nasty. The .308 and the shotgun would work well together. The best close and long range weapons ever devised.

"Doran, wedge that door up tight with a chair. Put some of those empty cans on top of the chair. If that cocksucker comes home, we'll know it in a hurry. Keep the shotgun right by you, topped off, safety off. I've got this .308 and two handguns." Rusty didn't think the guy would be here tonight, but if he did, they would have fire superiority. Maybe Shinda had killed them, who knows.

"We will leave at daylight, right?" Doran said.

"You can leave at daylight. I'm gonna have a nice breakfast and leave when I'm damn good and ready."

"What about Shinda, we will have to go back for him if he is not back by morning."

"Shinda can take care of himself; he'll catch up."

* * *

Doran had the door unwedged and was out of it at daylight. Rusty got up cursing and re-secured the door. He needed more rest. What was the hurry. Let it warm up some. Having the .308 gave him a lot of confidence. Let the little fucker go. He would be on a tear with that pump in his hand. And Rusty would have one more man backtrailing for him. He knew Doran would head east at the fork, going back looking for Shinda. Rusty was headed west. He wondered where that guy's four wheeler was. Then it hit him. "That's where it is," he whispered. He got up immediately.

Chapter 27

FORCED MARCH

Holly felt like she had been asleep five minutes when Ab woke her up. He handed her a water bottle. "We didn't eat much yesterday. Drink as much as you can. I got to keep you hydrated."

Ab was taking down the tent before she was even out of it. It was pitch black out, darker than when they had camped.

"Why's it so much darker?"

"Weather coming in, probably going to snow today. Put that gore-tex jacket on. I want to be moving in five."

"How far are we going?"

"Til we get to that four wheeler, or get into a pitched battle and get murdered."

"Thank you for that frank assessment. Nothing like starting off the day scared shitless," she thought. "So how far is it to that four wheeler?"

"I don't know. You ask too many questions."

Holly decided she should leave him alone, just follow him and try to stay off his feet. "Grumpy SOB," she said under her breath.

"What'd you say?"

"Nothing, Love. Ready when you are."

The only noise she heard all morning was the sound of mud squashing on the downstep, sucking on the upstep. It was dark and she couldn't see. After a while she just put her head down and trudged. Her feet were really hurting her now, and she knew she was going downhill fast. She had trouble keeping up from the start. The three miles were hard, and there was one scary incident when a huge animal jumped up and busted through the brush. Ab drew his .45 instinctively. Holly fell down in the mud, scared and exhausted.

Ab recognized what it was and turned around, not finding her for a second. "Moose. What the hell are you doing?"

"Practicing ducking."

"Good job."

Five minutes later he stopped her again. They were on the trail to the cabin. He checked the trail going west and north. Holly could see the relief on his face. "They went to the cabin. Both of them. We're past them now. We need to pick up the pace and get to the four wheeler."

It was getting light and Holly started seeing flakes of snow landing on Ab's pack. He really had a strong pace going now and she was fighting to keep up. She began falling back, and after an hour, had to call ahead. Snow was starting to accumulate on the trail now.

"Ab."

He stopped and turned quickly, Holly now forty yards behind. He walked back to her.

"I'm sorry, Holly. I was kind of in my own little world there. Too fast?"

"Yeah, I just can't keep up. I'm really tired, Ab. Between yesterday and today, I just don't know."

"About two more miles, then a half mile up the drainage and we'll be at the four wheeler."

"My feet hurt so bad, Ab. It just hurts to walk." She was almost crying now, really giving out fast. Ab was worried. Now he didn't know if he could get her there. He was pushing her too hard. Ab held her and hugged her tight.

"I'm sorry, baby, I'm just trying to get us out of this mess. I've been too hard on you. Too hard all morning. I'm sorry."

Holly was crying now. The emotional strain of the whole ordeal broke open and she couldn't hold it back anymore. Ab stood there in the snow, holding her up, feeling the soft crying turning into sobs. Ab thought it was some kind of post-traumatic stress thing. When it looked like they would make it and the worse stress had passed, she had just let go. But he did need to get her moving again, or at least over in the bush off the trail. It was well past daylight now, and the other two might be on the move, coming their way. They just couldn't stop. All Ab could think about was that four wheeler and getting to it. The weather was already bad, and getting to Jatahmund by four wheeler would take six or eight hours, depending on how many times they got stuck. His mind was made up. He would not spend another night out here. That quad was the key to their making it through the day.

"It's my fault, Ab, all my fault. I never should have got on that plane." She was crying, sobbing, and holding on to him. "I got you in all this mess because I'm stupid. My whole life is stupid; it always has been. Every day of it. And now I've brought it on you."

"Hey, Holly, you know what I think?"

She was crying, shaking her head. "What?"

"I think love can't have a bad day. Come on, we'll walk together." He put her arm around his shoulder and started her down the trail.

Chapter 28

TRACKING

Doran felt good with the pump shotgun. He had on the man's clothes and he was comfortable again. He was well rested and well fed. He was eager to find Shinda and see if he had found them and killed them. But he had made his mind up. He would stay out here til he knew they were dead, or he was dead. They had killed his little brother, and he would not leave until it was avenged. Shinda would not either.

Doran wanted to find Shinda and tell him about the cabin. They could stay there until it was done. The man and woman would come back to the cabin It was just a matter of time. And he would be there waiting, with the shotgun.

Doran made it to the fork in under an hour. It had started to snow. Just as he turned to go east, he saw the tracks. He turned around and looked west down the trail. They had been here. They had passed in the night. He looked carefully at the smaller bootprints. His brother's boots. He was in a full rage now, looking down at his brother's foot prints made by the woman. He would kill her this day. Kill the man. Kill both of them for this. Doran started to run down the trail, heading west.

* * *

Rusty was packing. He would find the four wheeler up that drainage. The mountain man had climbed the ridge, somehow. It was the only way he could have gotten to the crash that fast. Then he had to go east because he could not get the woman back down the cliffs. He would have driven the quad as far up as he could, until it got too steep. It would be sitting there; he knew it would. He just had to get there, find it, and he was home free. If there was no key, he would hot-wire it. It was coming together now. His two maniacs were out there, hunting the man and woman down, and he would be getting away. With any luck, he might be on a plane by tomorrow.

* * *

It was slow going. Holly's feet were in bad shape. Ab was half carrying and half dragging her along, moving now at a snail's pace. It took another hour to cover a mile, the snow coming down at blizzard strength now. Ab had Holly calmed down, but she was still fragile. He wanted to hide her off the trail and go get the quad. But if they came along before enough snow fell, they would know from the track that he had gone on alone and put her in the bushes. He couldn't leave her anyway, not now. They would just have to make it somehow.

They drug along for another forty-five minutes and finally arrived at the drainage. Ab was almost carrying Holly now, her feet useless.

"Holly, sit down here, baby. I've got an idea. You've got to be strong for me. Can you do that and do what I say?"

"I can, Ab, I will."

"I want you to do two things, but I've got to try and hide you first. You'll have to be without me for thirty minutes while I go get the quad. But first, I'm going to set a little surprise up for these boys. I want you behind this big rock up here." He helped her up the drainage for thirty yards to a wall of rocks that had piled up from rolling down the hill over the years. "Nobody can see you here. Just stay still and be quiet. Watch the trail, but stay down where no one can see you. I'll be back as quick as I can."

Ab hid his pack in the rocks and headed across the trail to the south. The Snag Creek drained into a small lake a hundred yards away. Ab found his way up to a big spruce tree on the south side of the lake. He got six Connibear 330 traps off a nail where he and Bearman kept them for trapping beaver. Holly watched him as he came back up on the trail, hauling all kinds of metal contraptions. He went 100 yards back down the trail to the east, setting traps in the middle of the trail. He finished and walked back over to her.

"All right, I got to go get the four wheeler. It's steep as hell, about a half mile. I'm going to run the whole way, love, as fast as I can, and drive like a maniac back down. I don't think you'll see anybody, but if you do, just stay out of sight. Those traps will be covered in five minutes with this snow. I put six of them right together. They'll break a leg or an arm instantly. Give me a kiss." She kissed him and touched his cheek, and he was gone.

* * *

Doran ran the first half mile. The snow was coming down hard now, as hard as he had seen it in the mountains of Pakistan. He knew they weren't that far ahead. Their tracks were filling with snow quickly, but were still easy to see. He slowed to a fast walk now. He would catch them, the woman for sure. He would blow her blood and brains into the white snow. Then he would hunt the man down. He would find Shinda, and they would celebrate.

After a mile, he saw the drag marks. She was not walking very well. They had to be moving slow now, maybe stopped ahead on the trail somewhere. He could only see a hundred yards in front of him now, the snow coming hard from the west into his face. Doran slowed down and got the gun up in front of him. He would be ready when he saw them. It wouldn't be long.

He came around a bend in the trail, and up ahead he could barely make out the huge drainage to the south. Then he heard a noise and stopped. It was getting louder, and he recognized it as a vehicle. It was high above him, coming downhill fast. Doran started running again as hard as he could.

* * *

The sound of the four wheeler lifted Holly's spirits. He was coming back. She was safe. She stood up and hobbled to the trail to be ready for Ab when he got there. She turned and looked back up the drainage. Ab was getting close, but the snow was heavy and it was hard to pick him out. Finally she could see him, spinning left and right, kicking up gravel, and she thought he might flip it with so much speed.

When he was twenty yards from her, she heard the first shotgun blast, spun and ducked at the same time, almost falling. She could see the man, running hard, shooting from the hip, shotgun pellets kicking up snow in front of her.

Ab braked hard and spun the quad's rear onto the trail, the front facing west. He yanked Holly onto the back with his right hand, and she grabbed his coat and held on. A blast of mud and snow from the shotgun pellets spraying the ground hit her in the face. Ab was back on the throttle now, giving it hell.

Holly was looking back and saw the man falling and heard the screams. The gun was flying forward out of his hand, and she heard the sequence of the traps going off. One-two, one-two-three. Both of his legs, then both of his arms and his face. It was Ab Bailey's signature shot sequence. She had heard it before. This time, he did it without a gun.

Chapter 29

THE OBJECTIVE

Rusty was in his pre-maneuvers soldier routine now. Just like when he was a young man with his squad. He was packing up quickly, efficiently, making snap decisions about food, clothing, and equipment. It wasn't just wandering through the bush anymore, like the lost children of Israel. He knew good and damn well where the promised land was. It was high up on that drainage. He was a soldier again with an objective to take. He shouldered the pack, grabbed the .308, and then thought about one last thing. He turned and walked over to the woodstove. Come on back home, motherfucker, and try and live happily ever after with your new bitch, he thought. Rusty tossed a burning stick of poplar on each bunk. Nobody would be chasing him with long guns today, not these anyway.

He was an hour behind Doran, but he was moving fast now. Good rest and good food gave him his strength back. But mostly it was the surge of energy brought on by knowing where you are going, exactly what you are going to do. He would get the four wheeler and go west on the trail as hard as he could. It would have to go north somewhere; it had to hook up with a road.

Rusty was shocked when he got outside and saw how hard it was snowing. That might be good, he thought, good cover. He wasn't hunting anyone, so anything that helped with his stealth couldn't be bad. He had a tent and a sleeping bag. Let it snow, let it snow. He turned back at the edge of the lake. Huge orange flames were already licking up the sides of the cabin walls. The whole structure would be gone in thirty minutes, just a red tin roof on the ground. He moved on, headed for the fork. It took him another forty minutes. The snow was four inches deep and the prints were vague, but they were there, going west. It was confusing with the snow. He thought there might be more than one set, but could not tell. Not good—this was not good. Rusty picked up his pace, heading west fast now.

Rusty was trying to think it through, walking fast, head up one second watching the trail ahead, down the next, trying to decipher the quickly disappearing tracks. The snow was filling them in fast. Maybe Doran had hooked up with Shinda at the fork. Not likely. Shinda would need rest and food. They would probably have come back to the cabin. No, this was not good. Damn the man, he had gotten ahead, somehow. He would get the four wheeler and be gone.

Thirty minutes later, Rusty heard the noise in the distance. Shotgun blasts. Eight of them. They were faint, but there was no mistaking them. That could only mean one thing. Doran had seen the tracks, headed west, and caught them. He didn't hear any other gunfire, just a shotgun. But as faint as the noise was, Rusty knew he might not hear a .45 since it was a quieter gun. It got quiet again and he kept moving, still trying to figure it out. He was convincing himself as he went along. It had to be, it just had to. Doran got them. He saw the tracks, he snuck up from behind, quiet in the snow, and he did it. Fucked 'em, fucked 'em both to hell. Yes, it made sense now. He shot them, but he wouldn't stop firing, not that little maniac.

Rusty felt better. He may have just caught another break. He was almost running now. But he wanted to see it, verify it with his own eyes. He came around a corner and stopped, out of breath. Far down the trail he could just make it out. They were crumpled in the snow and Doran was bent down over them, tugging at their bodies. They were close to the drainage. Rusty would take Doran up the drainage with him. He would kill him as soon as he found the quad, and leave him there. Then he would be gone.

Rusty yelled out to Doran, and he stood up. But Doran was a bear. Rusty flipped the safety forward on the little Remington and centered the reticle on the bear's chest, taking the slack out of the trigger. As soon as his eye came off the scope, after recoil, he saw the instant collapse, the deflating effect of 2000 foot pounds of kinetic energy, delivered on point.

Rusty ran the bolt, got back on the bear, and held there. No movement. He did it out of habit from sniper school training. The first rule after the shot—bolt and reacquire the target.

Rusty relaxed and started walking toward the bodies. Where the hell is Doran. And in a few more steps, he saw Doran, or what was left of him. He looked up and saw the four wheeler tracks, already getting snowed in. "Cluster fuck. Total goddamn cluster fuck," he said.

Chapter 30

JATAHMUND

Ab didn't look back, didn't need to. He was punching through gears, revving it to the max before each shift, plowing up snow and mud, headed for the Chisana River crossing. It was five miles to the crossing. The Chisana wasn't bad with a solid gravel bottom. He would blow right through it. Then it was eight miles of high ground, up and down low rolling hills. The Stuver Creek crossing would be the worst, but he had the winch and he had a full tank of gas. By then he would be thirteen miles away. He didn't have to worry about Holly now, all she had to do was hang on, and she was doing that, squeezing him so hard he almost couldn't catch his breath. She had her head pressed against his back, her arms locked around him, and her hands in his coat pockets. Ab just felt freedom and power. That's what a four wheeler was.

It was freedom and power. It always did what you told it too, instantly.

Bearman always preferred horses for bush travel, but not Ab. He hated horses. They were stupid, in his opinion, and he found them clumsy and unsure of themselves. If they didn't have four feet, they would fall down every two minutes. And what kind of self-respecting animal would let you get on its back, stuff a bit in its mouth, and then do your bidding. They should call them husbands, not horses. Try that with a bull elk, a truly majestic animal. Domestication, who needed it? Not Ab Bailey.

Holly was in the clouds now, floating, flying and hanging on to something real and solid. Something she had never held on to before. She wanted Ab to go faster and to go forever. Up and down hills and across rivers with the snow falling and the white frosted trees and land flying by her. Just keep going until the next ice age--that's what she wanted.

Ab plowed into the Chisana hard, blasting up a spray of water ten feet high on each side of the quad. He almost choked it out, but downshifted, kept it moving, and showered the river with rocks going up the west side. They were up and down hills for the next hour and a half, Holly losing her stomach, then getting it back on the uphill. She couldn't see ahead and never knew what was coming, whether it would be turns or steep grades up or down. She just held on tight, watching the trees go by at breakneck speed.

The Stuver was muddy. Ab got the quad all the way down in first, but it was bogging, and finally stopped. He stood up on the quad and shook it hard from side to side, giving it gas and throwing up mud all over Holly's legs. He got off and started rolling out the winch line.

"Is this bad?"

"No, it's expected. Not a problem. We'll be out of here in a minute. We're okay now; we got enough distance on them. I just wanted to get here fast. We'll take it a little easier from now on. We'll have a lot more of this kind of crap to get through."

"How far to go?" she asked.

"Oh, let's see." Ab was fighting through the mud, hooking the winch line around a small spruce. "Hang on to the handle bars, Holly. Steer it for me." The quad crawled up out of the mud.

"Maybe fifteen miles to Lick Creek, then we go north past a lot of little lakes, about twenty miles to Jatahmund. So about thirty-five total."

"How long, you think?"

"Depends on the trail, the mud. But before dark if I've got anything to do with it."

It took seven more hours and six more winchings, and Holly was thinking that maybe the next ice age would be a tad too long to stay on the back of this thing. Her back was hurting from eight hours of constant bumping up and down. The snow had not let up all day. The exhaustion was piling up on her again.

Ab was back up to being Ab as far as Holly could tell. He was singular of purpose again. He only spoke when he would give instructions to Holly about driving the four wheeler while he was operating the winch or moving deadfall off the trail. At least she was learning to drive the thing. She would inch it forward until they were out of the current mess. Then Ab would get back on and drive hard where he could go fast, then slow it down through the bumps and the muck and the over-hanging limbs. They would go fast, then slow, then stop. It was off and on all day. But at least she didn't have to walk anymore. Her feet must look like hamburger meat, Holly thought.

Other than to reach back and touch her leg occasionally with his left hand, Holly wondered if Ab even knew she was back there. He seemed so concentrated on what he was doing. She noticed something about Ab that was different than the other men that had been in her life. For a while, with them, it was all about Holly. Then it stopped like someone shutting off a light switch. Ab even looked at her differently. Not as an object or a trophy, but just as a person he was experiencing his life with. Even when she had broken down on the trail this morning, he didn't get all emotional with her or caught up in it with her. He just got her going again. He dealt with whatever came along, whenever it came along, and didn't dwell on it when it was corrected.

Holly wondered if there might be a bad flip side to that persona. This man could probably just walk away at the end of the day and not look back. She was becoming attached to a man who might not be attachable. Holly bumped along all day behind Ab having these thoughts. Funny, now that she was past her fear of dying, she was beginning to have the fear of living again. With thirty-eight years of hard knocks under her belt, Holly thought she had men all figured out. Then along comes this enigma. That's what he is—an enigma.

What could a man who lived out here and lived Ab's lifestyle want or expect out of life? It couldn't be the same things Holly was interested in, she thought. Then again, she didn't know what she wanted out of life anymore. It was probably too late for children. She was free; she had money. She could do anything she wanted to do. What did Holly Allen want? This morning it was just to stop walking and get out of this mess. But as for the rest of it, she just wasn't sure. If he would even try it, could she make a life with this man? Just breathe, Holly, she thought. Just be a perfect leaf and bump along on this four wheeler with this man. The heck with the rest of it. That felt pretty good.

"There it is."

Holly could see the cabin now. It was big, and low. Smoke was rolling out of the chimney, and it sat on flat ground, one hundred yards from a huge lake. She saw three other smaller buildings and a corral with horses in it. This was lower flat land, and Holly could not see any big mountains. As they rolled into the yard, Holly saw a tall lean man leading two horses. He had a thick mane of curly blond hair, and he immediately reminded her of a bigger, tougher looking version of Ab, if that was possible. The man saw her now and she could see the look on his face, dumfounded. Ab leaned back to her.

"If you think I'm a hick, get ready to meet a real knuckle dragger."

Ab cut off the quad and the man just stood there, looking back and forth from Holly to Ab, hands on his hips. Then he gave Ab the one eye.

"Let me guess. We been up to something besides cabin maintenance." Then he looked at Holly. "God-damn hired help."

"Your damn cabin's in perfect shape, I think," Ab said. "Oh, uh, this is Holly Allen. Holly, meet the Bearman."

He stuck out his hand. "Jordy Kampet."

"Nice to meet you, Jordy."

"We need to help her inside. Her feet are in bad shape."

"Been having to kick him a lot, huh? Try a stick to the head next time."

"She's already tried that."

"Yep, me too. Too damn hard headed. Come on, let's go inside where it's warm. Meet the family. I got a feeling it's gonna take an entire bottle of whiskey to get to the bottom of this."

They helped Holly in, and she saw a small lean woman cooking over a propane stove.

"Lauren, we got company."

The small woman turned around and just froze in disbelief. Then she got her composure back. Holly studied the woman's face. It was a kind face, weatherbeaten and lean. These people were all so lean. Lauren looked over at Ab. "Hey, Ab."

Bearman chimed in. "Lauren, this is Holly Allen. Don't know much about her yet. Except that she's way too pretty for him, her feet hurt from kicking him, and she's got damn poor taste in men."

Lauren went over and took Holly by both hands, obviously a kind woman. "Don't pay any attention to him. What's wrong with your feet?"

"Oh, just too much walking, wrong shoes." She could see the curiosity in the woman's eyes, not being able to put this all together.

"Jordy, watch the stove, don't let that moose meat burn, turn those potatoes. I'm going to have a look at Miss Allen's feet."

Bearman went to the stove and started tending it. He looked sideways at Ab. "Always barking orders at me. It's improper shock collar training, that's all it is. Well, don't just stand there, Wildman, pour us all a cocktail. You know where it is."

Ab got everybody a drink and could now see just how blistered Holly's feet were. Lauren was washing them and putting medicine on.

Holly was looking around the cabin. There were three rooms besides the big room they were in with a huge woodstove in the middle. All the furniture looked homemade, rustic but comfortable, with cushions and pads on the sofa and chairs. Animal skins hung everywhere. There was a huge moose shoulder mount on one wall, a caribou on another. A grizzly bear rug was draped over a homemade coffee table.

Bearman was setting the table, putting the food out. The meat and potato dishes were steaming. He put a big wooden bowl full of salad on the table, and two bottles of wine.

"Let's eat."

Lauren helped Holly up and over to the table. "Sit here Miss Allen."

"Please call me Holly. Thank you so much."

"I'll get you a hot bath going after dinner."

Holly and Ab were both starving. She was winding down fast with the good food and the wine.

Ab started in on the story during dinner. Bearman and Lauren were fascinated, shaking their heads in disbelief. Holly was listening too. Ab didn't mention a word about their intimacy, discreetly going through the facts of the chase.

Bearman was shaking his head, leaning back in his chair, toothpick in his mouth. "So you got four out of five of 'em, huh?" He looked over at Holly. "He never could finish a job. Damn, I wish that Beaver was here."

Ab rememberd the moose hunters now. "When did they fly out?"

"Yesterday afternoon. Which was good, because I don't think this weather's gonna break for a while."

"Good bulls?"

"Oh hell, yeah," Bearman said. "One of 'em was a seventy incher. Just took us two days. Horsebacked over to Takomahto. It was more like shopping than hunting. Them bastards can be pretty dumb when they're rutting. You know, that pisses me off, that son of a bitch still out there. Probably laid up in my cabin."

Lauren was standing up. "I'm going to get Holly a bath ready. You and Ab can wash the dishes."

Bearman looked at Ab and shook his head.

"I know, I know, shock collar training," Ab said.

Bearman waggled his finger at Lauren. "I'm gonna get that thing back out."

* * *

Lauren stayed with Holly while she bathed. She was asking Holly questions ninety to nothing after she found out she was an actress. Holly could tell she didn't get a lot of female companionship. She wanted to know all about Hollywood. Every time Holly would try to ask Lauren about herself, she would wave her hand at her. "Oh, I just take care of a bunch of old hunters. You don't want to hear that stuff." But Holly did. She was fascinated by this lifestyle. It was like she had gone back in time 100 years. But it was more than that. She wanted to know more about Ab. Holly tried to ask her questions in a subtle way, but she knew Lauren's woman's intuition was picking up on it, already had.

"He's a nice looking man, Holly. He's different though. He studies Zen, but you may already know that. That bugs Jordy sometimes. But he has total respect for Ab. He calls him Wildman."

"Why?"

"Well, because he is. But so is Jordy. They're just alike. They should have been brothers. But you have to accept them like they are, Holly. They're in this country for a reason. They won't be told what to do. These are men who live life on their own terms. And this man who's after you, he got the worst break of his life when he crossed Ab Bailey. I'm really surprised he's still alive. Did it bother you watching Ab kill those men?"

Holly thought about the question. "Not one bit. And he's good at it. It's obvious."

"Oh yeah. Jordy says it all the time. What a natural born killer Wildman is. Jordy says he's better with a bow or a handgun than any man he's ever seen. I've seen men in camp who would outshoot Ab with a bow on a target, and then they totally choke in the field, under real pressure. But not Ab. Jordy says he's never seen Ab miss. Ask him about it."

"You and Jordy don't have any children?" Lauren hung her head, and Holly knew it wasn't a good subject. "I'm sorry, it's none of my business."

"No, no, it's all right. We had a little girl, but she died in a horse accident. It was harder on Jordy than me, I think. I can't have any more. But we're ok, we're doing fine. Let's get you dried off and into some of my clothes."

"He is a nice looking man, isn't he?" said Holly.

"Yes, he is. But be careful, Holly."

* * *

Bearman was washing, Ab was drying.

"What do you think, Bearman?"

"I don't know. I got to work this through my head. Not much we can do for a few days, until the weather breaks. He'll probably stay at that cabin til then. There won't be any flying for a few days, and it's almost impossible to get to Northway through the Muskegg Swamp before the freeze. So we either stay here or head out by quad or horse and try to kill him. But you're gonna need a couple of days off. You look whipped."

Ab grinned at him. "I'm fresh as a fucking Daisy."

"You're fresh all right," the Bearman said. He faced the bedroom door and called out, "Hey, Lauren, don't let out that bathwater." Then he turned back to Ab and said, "No, I think we should just stay right here for a couple of days. Maybe the weather will break. Even if he was moving this way now, it would take him three days. Hell, he's fifty miles from here. Go take a bath. We'll figure it out in the morning."

Holly sat on the couch and had a drink with Lauren and Bearman while Ab bathed. Bearman wanted her perspective on the shootings.

"It was just so fast, Jordy. It's his face more than anything. That concentration and that confidence. I mean, it's just palpable. You just see that look, and then about a second later people are dead."

"He is fast with that four by five," said Jordy.

"What?"

"His .45."

"Oh. You talk like he does."

"He really just brings that for the drive up. Has to hide it to get through customs. He usually doesn't carry it in the bush. It's a little light for most applications up here. He is a killer though. And he's fast as greased lightning. He's fast at everything."

"I noticed he's fast with that tongue when he wants to be," Holly said.

"Oh, yeah," Bearman said. "He can be quite the smart ass."

"You should know," Lauren said.

"Easy there, woman."

Ab came back in the room and immediately sat down by Holly. Bearman picked up on it and started grinning at Ab.

"You're just glad to see me, I guess," Ab said.

"I'm just glad not to have to smell you."

Lauren was shaking her head. "Come on, Holly, we'll leave these two to their juvenile wit and get your bedroom ready."

Bearman was still grinning. "You can take that northwest bedroom, Wildman."

Ab had his head bent over, scratching it. He didn't want to make eye contact. "Well, I might just, uh," he was pointing back toward Holly's room.

"You dirty rotten hoor." Bearman was laughing. "You are fast at everything."

* * *

Ab opened Holly's door and stuck his head in. "Hey, I can sleep down in the other room if you want me to."

"Shut up and get in this bed."

They only made love once, and Ab noticed it was different. Holly kept his body close to her, their kissing was more intense, and she wouldn't let go afterwards. She was tired, but she wanted to talk. More than that, she wanted Ab to talk.

"They are really nice people, Ab. Lauren is a caring woman, I can tell. She's kind."

"Yes they are. They have always been good to me."

"What happened to their little girl?"

"Oh, it was just a horrible accident, Holly. She was four. Her name was Lindy. She was so pretty. Blond and full of life. She could already ride a horse better than me. Of course, that's not saying much. Anyway, they had this huge draught horse named Tak, and he just loved that little girl. You should have seen it, Holly. She would lead him around the yard by a halter. He had to put his head all the way down to the ground for her to walk him. But he would do it. Anyway, she went out to see him one morning in his stall, and the wall was not in good shape. She got up next to it. Of course, Tak wanted to be close to her, and he leaned against it too hard, and it broke and came over on her and killed her. Jordy can't forgive himself for it. He won't even talk about it. But they've moved on. It's been four years now."

They laid quiet for a few minutes, Holly playing with Ab's hair, but he could feel something in the air. It would have to be dealt with at some point.

"Ab, what did you mean today, on the trail, when I was so upset. You said, 'Love can't have a bad day.'"

"Well, you were so upset. You were upset because you were scared and you were hurting. But you transferred all that to your entire past, or what you think your past was. I just saw it as a problem that we had, and we had it together. For five days, your problems were mine, and mine were yours, which brought a bond of love between us. And nobody could take that away from us. They might have killed us, but they couldn't take that away. It was ours. It was our day. How could it be bad? The problem that you had at the time had nothing to do with the emotions you were pouring out. All the other times things were bad out there, I saw you deal with them as they occurred. Then, on the trail, with nothing to deal with but your pain, you started transferring in your brain. It's what we've talked about before. No reason to worry about things you can't control, or things that have already occurred in your life which you have no control over either. I think if you had not done that, and just realized you had a walking problem, you wouldn't have gotten so emotional. You were walking along in a form of mind slavery, and I just wanted to bring you back to the house of truth."

"I don't know what the truth is anymore, Ab. I certainly don't know anything about a house of truth."

"The house of truth is the absolute, Holly. It's the here and now. It's an understanding and a refusal of the transposition of the human map of being onto the real world."

"What does that mean?"

"Well, let me give you an example. Where are we, Holly?"

"In a cabin in Alaska, I think."

"But think of it this way, Holly. If you walk out the door and head east, you won't ever see the Canada and Alaska border. You'll eventually walk right into Canada, and without human intervention, you would never know it. Same for California and Nevada. Without human busybody mapmaking, it all just looks like contiguous land. When you're on that jet home, look down and figure out where Canada ends and the U. S. starts. You can't do it. Because the world is not a map. Our brain is the only mapmaker. Mapping is useful, but it's not the house of truth, Holly. No one from outer space will ever look down and say, 'That's Mississippi and that's Alabama.' But when I'm on my way home and I cross by that sign that says I'm now in Alabama, it gives me a feeling that I'm home. But it's not a true feeling, Holly, because it's just an arbitrary line. You can walk between Alaska and the Yukon all day and you will never see a line. So I guess what I'm saying is to quit looking for boundary lines that aren't really there other than in your mind."

"So just forget about the past, live in this moment, or breath, as you call it, and refuse to accept someone else's artificial boundaries. Is that the Ab Bailey Zen path to freedom?"

Ab laughed at her and kissed her. "Why don't we call it Holly Allen's path to freedom."

"I wouldn't mind a little freedom from this old world, Ab."

"No, no, no. You're missing the point. It's freedom from you, Holly. Freedom from your own cage, not the world. The 'old world,' as you call it, is not your enemy. It is you, and you are it. It's like when I hear preachers in organized religions tell people they have to find God. That's so ludicrous. God is the world. He's here all the time. You don't have to look for God. He's every breath you take. It's not a question of finding him; it's how not to lose him. That's the hard part."

"You make it sound so simple, Ab. But you're not going to convince me that life is as easy as rolling along thinking about my breathing. It doesn't work that way. You know that."

"And that's the problem, Holly. When you quit trying to analyze it and figure out how it works, and finally just realize that it does work and that that's all you need to know, you will begin to move right along with it, most of the time."

"What are we gonna do, Ab?"

"We'll figure it out. It'll be ok. Hey, look at us. Laying in a cushy bed. No bad guy problems tonight. We can just relax for a couple of days, get you rested up good. There will be a plane in within a week with supplies. Bearman will need to ship all these hides and horns out. I mean, if you're in a hurry to go, we can probably horseback it to town, but that Muskegg Swamp is tough until it freezes up."

"I'm not in that big of a hurry, Ab, and that's not what I was talking about?"

"Yeah, I know what you were talking about. Heck, I don't know. You live in Hollywood, I live up here and in Alabama. Not exactly the same lifestyle. And you gotta be there to do those movies. Hey, we'll always have Paris."

"That's not funny, Ab,"

"I know it. Let's just take it a day at a time. I might show you a few things about a .45 tomorrow. My training rates are very reasonable."

"I just bet they are."

"We could start working on a down payment right now."

"I've already bought every class you offer."

"Tips are always welcome."

"I'm not gonna get out of this, am I?"

"You should have let me go to sleep when you had the chance. Come here."

* * *

Ab got up when he smelled the coffee and left Holly in bed sound asleep. Bearman was looking out the window, drinking coffee, watching it snow. Ab poured himself a cup and walked over.

"Pretty noisy in there last night. You trying to rescue that woman or kill her?"

"Other way around, buddy," said Ab.

"Ho, ho, ho. He's so damn irresistible."

But Ab didn't seem like he was in a joking mode this morning. Bearman looked at him. "You guys had a pretty tough go of it out there, didn't you?"

"It got pretty intense a couple of times. We're out of it now, I guess."

"Looks to me like you've just got into it, Wildman."

"I don't know, Bearman." Ab was squeezing his temples. "How can a man's life get so complicated in five days?"

"Oh, it's easy. Especially when you're out there together, just each other to depend on. You can push a year into a week pretty fast. It don't go by the clock, you know."

"I guess."

"Besides, she seems like a pretty good fit for you. Lauren's been worried about you for a while now. You spend too much time alone. This might be good for you."

"So what, I'm just gonna go to L.A. and hang around? I mean this woman's got a life, a very different life than I do. She's sure as hell not gonna go to Alabama and hang around a deer camp and shooting range with me all winter. It'll be over when she leaves, Bearman. That's all there is to it."

"We'll see about that."

"So when you got a plane coming?"

"It'll be a few days. Maybe longer with this weather." Bearman was looking out the window again. "I wonder if that bastard is coming this way yet. He's gonna have to, sooner or later."

"Yeah, he might be by here before you can get word back to town," Ab said.

"I almost hope he does. I think we should deal with it, not the law. Those guys couldn't find a bull moose in a basement. Anyway, it bugs the shit out of me, some guy running around my concession, trying to kill my people. And a fucking kidnapper, too. We won't have to start worrying until tomorrow though. But going out there after him would be stupid. I mean he could bypass us and get to these women. I can't let that happen. We'll think it out during the day."

"Lauren still asleep?"

"Yeah. She busts her ass when those hunters are here. Let 'em both sleep. They need it. So when are you headed south?"

"I don't know. Might take the plane with Holly, or the next one. Yul D will kill me if I'm not home by October 15th. He booked the whole camp with bow hunters, and he don't know shit about bow hunting. Good time of year to hit the Alaska Highway anyway. Just get the old truck in Northway, be home in two weeks. Right on time."

* * *

Holly walked into the room, came straight over to Ab and gave him a kiss. She looked at Bearman. "I don't suppose there's any reason to try and keep secrets from you."

"I make it my business to know everything that goes on in my concession. I don't have to like it, but I do need to know it."

"What's not to like?" Ab asked.

"A desperate woman being taken advantage of by the likes of you."

Holly poured herself a cup of coffee. "You two never stop, do you?"

"So what do you think of our little neck of the woods, Miss Allen?"

"It's beautiful. Harsh, but beautiful. I think I might enjoy it more if people weren't trying to kill me."

"Well, make him leave you alone at night. I tried to get him to sleep in another room. By the way, should be a plane here in three or four days." He looked at Ab. "If that damn Chicken Bob would get off his ass and fix my Beaver, I'd be saving a lot of money on these damn plane ferries."

Holly looked at both of them. "Chicken Bob?"

"Oh, uh, you're gonna have to get used to Bearman speak. He puts the town that people are from in front of their name, helps him keep them straight. Like, uh, Althabasca John, or Clear Prairie Don, Boundary Pete, Northway Jack. He needs all the help he can get, being mentally challenged and all. I guess you would have to be Hollywood Holly."

"What about Ab, Bearman, no town name for him?"

"Nah, he's just the Wildman. Besides, no town would have him."

Lauren came in the room and immediately started the stove. "Good morning, all."

"It's about time you got up and fed the king and his minions, woman." Bearman walked around behind and started pinching her rear.

"Stop it, Jordy, we got guests. Have you checked on that mare, yet?"

"I was just about to go do that."

"Well, shoo, scat, go do it."

"Come on, Ab, let's go to the barn and check on a female, one with some manners."

Holly came over to the stove. "Let me help."

"Oh, I got it. Just enjoy your coffee. How did you sleep last night?"

"Oh, it was wonderful, Lauren. I was so tired. Ab only let me sleep four hours the night before. I almost didn't make it yesterday. I think Ab carried me more than I walked for the last mile."

"Holly, they'll push you when nobody's after you. They just go so hard in the bush. They forget everybody else can't do it. I hate to walk with Jordy. They're just tough men, and they can't understand why everybody else is not. Some of these fat guys come in camp and Jordy just has fits about it. He gives me an earful at night. Him and Ab work so hard to get them a good animal. But if a guy can't climb the hill to shoot the sheep, he goes home empty. Of course, he goes home and blames the outfitter for a bad hunt, and then Kampet and Sons Outfitting gets a bad reputation. It just makes Jordy so mad. But Ab was good to you out there, wasn't he?"

"Oh, he was, Lauren. He was suspicious at first, I could tell. I mean he didn't know what was going on. He just walked into a bad situation and dealt with it."

"I bet it was a bad situation for those guys after he got there."

"He scared me too, at first. Those blue eyes are pretty intimidating. And he killed those men so fast. I thought he might shoot me too when he first walked up. But then he just walked over to me and spit out some of that nasty tobacco juice. He called me Pocohantas."

"Why?"

"I guess it was my outfit. I had these brown blankets wrapped around me. I was just freezing to death. But I gotta tell you, Lauren, I spent two of the best days of my life with that man out there."

"What are you gonna do, Holly?"

"I don't know, Lauren, I don't know."

Lauren had the food on the table when Ab and Bearman came in.

"How is she, Jordy?"

"Oh, she's fine. She won't deliver for another week. Damn good female. Let me poke and prod all over her and not one word of backtalk. You ought to think about that."

"Go get the butter."

"So Ab says you're gonna get a shooting lesson today, Hollywood."

Ab grinned. "I told you he would come up with a name for you. A condensed version of Bearspeak."

Ab only had two extra boxes of .45 ammo. He took Holly out to Bearman's rifle range and set up a piece of cardboard. He spent an hour making her handle the gun before he even loaded it. Grip, stance, sight alignment, trigger control. He kept barking orders at her, making her do things over and over again. Screaming at her about keeping her thumb on top of the safety, how to load it, how to rip the slide, how to clear malfunctions, press checks and transitions, just so much stuff to learn.

"Gosh, Ab, I never knew there was so much to this. I thought you just pointed the thing in the general direction and pulled the trigger."

"Well, that's a good way to make a lot of noise, Holly, but it might not solve our problem. We want to get good hits, and get them fast, faster than the other guy. It's all about speed and accuracy. You ought to see some of the world class guys I shoot against in competition. It doesn't even look real."

"I thought you were world class."

"Oh hell no. There's lots of guys faster than me."

"I don't know, Ab. I don't think I can do this."

"Sure you can. I mean you can learn. Think of this as a martial art, Holly. In fact, I think it's the ultimate martial art. You've just stepped into the dojo, and I can't make you a black belt in one day. I can give you the tools. If you practice, you'll get there, but it will take time, and dedication. And I always think these things are more important for a woman than a man. I mean, think what a great equalizer that is for a woman. It doesn't matter how big or how bad the guy is. You can have the upper hand. It's within your power to do that, Holly. And the feeling you'll get from it is not that you're some kind of bad-ass. It's a feeling of confidence and freedom. People always say you're paranoid if you carry a gun, but it's just the opposite. It's freedom from paranoia."

She knew he was right. It was easy to be smug and condescending when you were in a warm, fuzzy, safe place. But the world wasn't always so warm and fuzzy. She knew that now.

Ab got her on live fire drills, but there was just so much they could do with 100 rounds. He stayed after her about trigger control most of all. Holly got frustrated. She would line up the sights like he said; then when she pulled the trigger, the bullet hole would be a foot off.

"What am I doing wrong, Ab? I had the sights right on the dot."

"You did, right up until the time you jerked the trigger. At this distance, five yards, sight picture is not that crucial, but trigger control is always at a premium."

"How do you do it so fast and good?"

"It's all muscle memory. To be honest, at this distance, and even further, I'm not even looking at my sights. It's more like I'm looking through them. It's ninety-five percent trigger control, sweetheart, and it just takes a lot of practice."

She was getting better by the time they finished. Holly felt like a new door had opened for her, one she intended to walk through.

* * *

Bearman was fleshing a grizzly cape when Holly and Ab finished. Holly wanted to see what it was all about. She walked over to him. "Why do you have to do that?"

"Keep the hair from slipping. I'll get it fleshed, turn the nose and ears, split the lips, do the feet, and then I'll stretch it and salt it down. It will last for years like that. When it gets to the tannery, they'll rehydrate it, clean it up and tan it. Then you got a nice flat skin. The owner can then have a rug done, or a full body mount, whatever he wants."

"What does the salt do?"

"It draws the moisture out of the hide, which sucks it down on the hair follicles, so the hair won't fall out. Nothing worse than having a boinking rug with bald spots on it." He paused and grinned at Holly. "So why didn't you shoot him when you had a chance?"

"I don't think I could hit him yet. I need to practice," said Holly.

Bearman looked at Ab. "So, what are you guys gonna do this afternoon?"

"Oh, I don't know. I thought we might, uh, go take a nap."

"Nap my ass. I think there's gonna be a Wildman in Hollywood, that's what I think." Then Bearman broke down at his own joke.

Ab was asleep five minutes after they made love. He could be so energized and so focused one minute, Holly thought, and so lazy and carefree the next. The man just couldn't stay awake after sex. Small price to pay for those performances though. They both woke up about an hour later.

Holly was pushed up against his back, playing with his hair. "Did you say you were going back to Alabama soon, Ab?"

"Yeah, I got to. I promised Yul D I'd be back before the start of bow season. He needs help with training classes too. I'll be teaching some of those. Probably shoot a few matches, stuff like that. Yul D's not so young anymore. He sort of wants me to get this Alaska stuff out of my head and come take over the business."

"Are you going to?"

"Eventually. I mean, I'll keep coming up in the summer and early fall for a few more years. I just love it too much. I love to be around these people, especially that crusty old son of a bitch. And it's so damn hot in Alabama. I'm always ready to get the hell out of there by June. That's when Bearman wraps up his spring bear hunts in Alberta, and him and Lauren move up here for the fall and winter. He traps in the winter. It's easy to get around up here after it freezes. They do it by Ski-Doo. You can be to Northway in two hours."

"How do you get home?" she asked.

"Float plane to Northway, just like you're gonna take. I've got my truck there. Got all my camping stuff there. I'll just take off down the old Alaska Highway. You'll either have to take a plane to Tok or Anchorage, I don't know which. It will be jet service then. They should get you to L. A. in a day. We'll probably fly to Northway together, but I hate to fly."

Holly laughed. "You're afraid to fly? I love to fly. Well, I used to."

"I'm not exactly afraid of it. I'm just never comfortable. It's a control thing."

"Ab Bailey's got to be in control. We know that."

Tone of voice. Tone of voice. Get ready, buddy.

"Ab, we been dancing around this for two days. I don't know how to get past it other than to talk about it. What about us?"

"What about us?" Ooh, that wasn't good, he thought.

"Damn you, Ab. You'll just walk away from it. You'll get in that little Zen trickbag of yours, and that will be the end of it. I know you. I haven't known you long, that's true. But we got something here, Ab. Or at least I do. And it's something I've never had before."

Ab rolled over and looked at her. So beautiful. The kind of woman that a man drives down the highway and thinks about. The kind of woman that always seems to be on some other guy's arm. On the arms of some dickwad that looks cool on the outside, but there's no man inside, just a waste of fucking skin. And that's why it wouldn't work. Ab didn't even want to go there. He didn't want to think about it anymore.

"What are you gonna do, Holly? Come live in a deer camp with me? You gonna live out here with me? How long do you think I would last in Los Angeles, California? I'll tell you. Almost as long as you would in my world. I mean that's it. End of story."

"You're a cold son of a bitch, Ab Bailey."

Ab put on his clothes and went outside. He was pretty steamed. Not mad at Holly, but mad at himself, mad at the situation. He wanted her—that was easy to see. But he wasn't a kid anymore, or one of those "love conquers all" optimists. He wanted to get his gun and go storming through the bush, find that fucking man who was lurking out there and blast his goddamn spine out. Just take this out on somebody.

He noticed Bearman on his hands and knees, rubbing salt on the bear hide, looking at him.

"Trouble in Paradise?"

"Aw hell, I don't know."

"Did we get the 'what are we gonna do now' confrontation, Wildman?"

"What are you, a mind reader?"

"I got the same make and model in the house, buddy. I know how the machinery works."

"Well, you better enlighten me, Bearman. I think mine just threw a rod."

"That's what got you in this mess, throwing your rod around. Hell, put her in the truck. Take her to Alabama."

"I don't think that's gonna work," said Ab.

"That's your problem. You think too much. You always have."

It wasn't his thinking, Ab knew. It was the one thing he just couldn't work out. The one thing he couldn't get his arms around. A real relationship with a woman. He had thought about it a lot. He never meshed with his first wife, or a lot of other women, for that matter. Divorce didn't mean anything pro or con for Ab. Marriage ceremonies didn't cut it either. Ab was pretty much against ceremonies in general. Any kind of pomp and circumstance turned him off. Besides, he had been in more meaningful relationships with women he didn't get married to. To Ab, it didn't matter about the finality of the ceremony, or the legal status according to the law. It didn't bother him one bit that Holly had been married three times.

It was just the relationship part he didn't get right. She obviously hadn't either. For that fact, millions of married people never get it right. Even people who have been married for a lifetime. Just saying you are married, or staying married forever, doesn't define a relationship. People who are miserable sometimes stay together because they have become comfortable with their misery. It's just a constantly changing beast. Staying the course is always tough. And Ab Bailey knew that he found it harder than most people. It was the one issue on which he did not trust himself. And with two totally different lifestyles, staying together with Holly after this ordeal was over would be a monumental and potentially painful task.

But take it or leave it, the thing had started itself up. And it was just like Bearman said in his eloquent way: it was basically Ab's doing that cranked it up. Maybe he was wrong in his thinking, but Ab always believed it was harder to relate to women as you went up the masculinity scale. He had known lots of what he called "metrosexual" men in law school. They always seemed to get along fabulously with women. Men who never went outdoors or shot guns or gutted animals. They wore khakis and sweaters and stood around at social functions drinking white wine and just chatting it up with women. They understood female stuff and the feminine way of thinking. Not Ab Bailey. He didn't give one shit about shopping or new clothes styles, or any of that other hooey they were always gabbing about. When he rarely went to one of those functions, he just stood around with a beer in his hand, improperly dressed in his blue jeans and cowboy boots, being shunned by the beautiful people in record numbers. He got those looks too from people who seemed to him to be thinking, "Sorry we didn't put a tire on a chain over here in the corner for you." Something for the Neanderthal to entertain himself with.

The flip side was that Ab wasn't going to apologize to anyone for being the man he was. It wasn't his fault that he labeled bullshit "bullshit." He just had a low tolerance for what he considered nonsense. Or maybe he was just plain inflexible. What he wanted to do was get back to breathing, to being here and not in some fantasy argument with himself about what he was or what he did or didn't need. It was always the hard part of living. The self-assessment. And outside of this relationship ape on his shoulders, he did a pretty good job. Of course, unless he became a eunuch, it would always nag him. Basic animal needs. The superstructure of existence. Probably the cause of more grief, joy, and the exchange of money than anything else on the planet. He doubted if even the greatest Zen masters didn't have to grapple with it from time to time. Even the deer and the moose fought like hell about it during the rut. Apparently, Ab thought, you had to be a self-pollinating plant not to have trouble with sex and the opposite sex from time to time.

Chapter 31

THE WALK

Rusty stood there a while, looking at Doran's mutilated body, the bones of his left leg exposed where the bear had been feeding. The smaller bones, just above the ankle, had been broken by the trap. The other leg had been caught by the knee. Both of his hands had gone straight down, trying to break his fall, and both arms were snapped halfway between the wrist and the elbow in the second row of traps. But it was his face that got to Rusty, smashed in by the force of the metal jaws, pushing his top teeth out three inches too far, in a macabre way. Doran's face made Rusty think of some weird mix of a Jerry Lewis movie and a horror show at the same time.

He knew now that Shinda was dead. Bad luck, that's all it was. And Rusty knew now that it wasn't going to get any better for him. The jig was up. There was only one way out and it was down the same trail that the mountain man had taken. He would run into the law or this sick trap-setting cunt somewhere on this trail. He made up his mind. He would just walk. He would walk all day and all night. He would walk 'til he fell down, and then he would get up and walk some more. If he met a human, any human, he would kill him then and there, on the spot, and he would keep walking. He would either walk out of this mess a free man, or he would die walking.

He had reached that point that other soldiers had. Outnumbered, or outgunned, the last man standing. Rusty would go down fighting. He didn't care anymore. His own death was inevitable. And it would be worth it to die if he could trade it for a chance to kill the mountain man. That would be glory.

He was just in another bad mess. Nobody to depend on but yourself, Rusty thought. And of course no one cared about him or what happened to him. But Rusty didn't feel sorry for himself. That was for suckers and weaklings. They would all care about what happened to the actress. It was the way of America. He had abandoned his country for that very reason. Every time some dumb ass took a shit in Hollywood, it was all over the news. But send a man out on a mission to fight and die for his country and it barely got a passing mention on a news channel. Rusty knew there were lots of men who were feeling like him these days. Why bother. The faggots and leftists all hated the military and any man who acted like a man to protect what he loved and cared about. He would advise every young man in America not to join up anymore. Let the assholes in New York and Hollywood and the politicians' sons go fight the next war.

It was why Rusty had no concern for the Allen woman. Gorgeous, living a privileged lifestyle, and she and her kind wouldn't give a real man like him the time of day. Killing her would be an emotionless event for Rusty. If he could just get to her. Then they could pour it all over the airways. They could whine and cry about her all over the U. S. At this point, he didn't even care if they plastered his face on TV. Being a bad man was the only way a man like him would ever get any recognition. It definitely didn't come from doing your duty. Scorned and fucked was all you got for that. He was living proof of it.

Outside of a few old army buddies, not a soul in the world knew what he had done for his country, much less cared. Like over in the Storm when he and his squad were HALO dropped into Indian country in the middle of the night. Setting up IED's to disrupt supply convoys going to resupply the Republican Guard troops. They were caught out in the open and ambushed by rogue villagers. Rusty and his boys kept them off for two days until a forty-man troop of the elite Republican Guard arrived. It was run and gun for twenty-four hours after that. The SAW completely disintegrated on them. They were left with two mags of ammo each for the M4's. They finally made a stand in a deep ravine late that evening. Must've taken out twenty-five Iraqis. Those hotdogs lost their nerve for a while. But Rusty lost three good men out of five.

He and his corporal ran for most of the night, then turned and waited until the cautiously advancing troop came inching up to a sand hill. He thought for sure that would be his last stand. But he had made it. He popped up over that dune and wasted ten of those boys in heartbeat, screaming and cursing through an entire magazine. He never even got grazed by a bullet. The five or six hostiles that were left made a hasty retreat and Rusty and his boy were on the move again, fast. He finally got clear enough to call for an extraction at 3:00 a.m. on the third day. He would never forget the sound of that Blackhawk chopping through the air, not putting lights on until Rusty hit his strobe when the bird was only two hundred yards out. He baled on that chopper and lay on his belly for the first forty-five minutes.

The entire mission had been considered a failure because they were outed by the villagers on the first day. But Rusty knew he was a hero. All it had ended up costing him was three good friends and a wife and child. His dead buddies' families got 12,500 dollars each in death benefits. People who were sitting in the World Trade Center doing nothing, who got killed, got almost a million dollars each from the government. No doubt about it, the United States had become one big politically correct fucked up place. Why any young man would volunteer to join the U. S. military was mind boggling.

It was all about Rusty now. He had learned his lessons the hard way. Sometimes he thought he was just stupid. If he had just been able to see the "me" mentality of the States twenty years ago and followed suit like all of the other cocksuckers out there, he could have saved himself a lot of grief. It was all running through his mind as he moved along in the snow. It was the Storm again, another last stand to be dealt with, and Rusty considered these enemies to be far more evil than the peasants he had faced overseas.

So he did what soldiers do. It was called the warrior mentality. That total, reckless disregard for a man's own life that got medals of honor penned on men's chests. He just wanted one more chance. One more chance to vanquish the foe. So he would walk. Just like his old boot camp sergeant used to say: "Transportation today, boys, will be by black Cadillac." Rusty started walking.

By the time it was dark, Rusty had crossed one wide river, covered miles of rolling hills, and made his way across a muddy creek. He saw different animals along the way, but no sign of a human. He was trudging through the snow, waiting on a trap to snap a leg bone in two, or a bullet to hit him in the chest. Nothing happened, so he just kept walking until his body gave out. It was not his mind, or his will. It was his legs. They gave up first. There was no use to keep falling.

Rusty struggled to get the tent up in the dark, but he managed it. He got inside, into the mountain man's sleeping bag, and ate some of the mountain man's food. He drifted off to sleep, a warrior still looking for a battle.

He was awake at daylight. He ate some more and drank water, trying to rehydrate so that his legs would not betray him today. He had his fighting edge, and he wanted to use it before it was gone. He packed up his camp and was moving again within an hour after daylight. It was still snowing, and walking was getting harder, trudging through the fresh powder. He only stopped one time before midday, to drink from a stream. Later in the afternoon, far down the trail, a moose cow stepped out, stopped, and stared at him. He would check the rifle again. It was close to 300 yards, so he got down in the prone position and held at the top of her neck. He could see her falling before he lost the scope to recoil, the neck broken by the slug. He knew the gun was sighted in for 200 yards now, with a ten inch drop at 300. He could hit a man at 400 with it, if he had a good rest, and the target stayed still.

By late afternoon Rusty was dragging. He was pulling himself along by sheer force of will. He was in the flatlands now, and couldn't see any mountains ahead.

He had no idea how far he had come, but guessed that it was over thirty miles. He finally sat down in the snow, opened the pack, and got something to eat. He made sure to stop every hour or so and drink from streams. Walking in the cold keeps a man from feeling his thirst, and Rusty knew that hydrating was the key to his stamina. He went for an hour after dark, plodding, body giving out again, and still no sign of anything human. There were no roads, no people, no lights. He wondered how any place left on earth could still be this uninhabited. It was just snow and land and animals, and a trail that went forever.

He began to think that maybe he had missed it, a trail or cutoff hidden by the snow. Perhaps he had passed it in the dark last night, or this evening. The legs were going again now. He would have to stop and rest, then get up and do it again in the morning. But just at that moment, Rusty picked up a smell. It was the smell of wood smoke.

Chapter 32

ACCEPTANCE

Dinner was tense. The friction in the air between Holly and Ab was palpable, to the point of embarrassment for everyone. It was like being at a dinner party with a mad couple, with a bone that couldn't be picked in public. So it just festered, right through the buffalo steaks and the wine and the blueberry pie. Bearman got up and went outside. Ab followed him.

"I'll be damn, it's clearing up."

"Yeah, Bearman, probably be good flying weather tomorrow. You think that Otter will be in?"

"No, he'll be backed up for a day or two. He'll have to ferry hunters out of Macauly's Camp first, before he brings a load in here."

"What you got coming?"

"Ah, the usual. Propane, gas, groceries. Some stuff Lauren wanted. Horse medicine. I don't know what else. You gonna fly out on this one?"

"No, not unless this Rusty character is dealt with first. I ain't leaving til that mess is cleaned up."

"He ain't going anywhere, Wildman. He's laid up in that cabin right now. Holly will have to go to the cops as soon as she gets to town anyway and tell 'em the story. They'll load up a couple of those fish cop helicopters and go out there and smoke his ass. It'll be over soon enough. Hey man, you did good. You saved a nice woman. Too bad you had to go through all that and then turn around and be a jackass to her."

"Now, wait a damn minute, Bearman. I mean, goddamn it, what am I supposed to do? You're supposed to be on my side."

"I am on your side, Ab. That's why I said it." He turned and went inside.

Ab stayed outside and had a dip. What the hell could he do? It was better to break it off now than watch some stupid long-distance relationship go down the toilet slow and painful. I've been through that shit before, he thought. If she had been some other woman, more on his level, more ordinary, he could see it. But this would end up bad. And he knew the truth. He wasn't trying to protect her from him. It was the other way around. He didn't trust that she could do it, love a hick like him. Oh sure, when you're stuck out here, living on blueberries and love, it's easy. But what happens when she gets back to her real life. "I thought you were flying to see me this weekend," he could hear himself saying, and then he could imagine her answer, "Well I can't, Ab. I got this premier, or party, or something. Maybe next month." Nope. He would not do it.

Lauren and Holly were washing dishes when Bearman came back in.

"What have you been doing out there, Jordy?"

"Oh, just talking to the Jackass. Weather's clearing. I think we'll see that plane in a couple of days."

"Why is he being like this, Jordy?"

"Well, Holly, you got to see it from Ab's perspective too. He's got a case of you, there's no doubt about that. And I don't have any doubt that if the continental U. S. fell off in the ocean tomorrow and you guys had to live up here, that it would be all peachy. But that's not the reality of it. He won't even try it with you in L.A. I know him too well. I know he's being the hardass here, but the ball's really in your court. What do you think, Lauren?"

"I think what I've always thought, Jordy. You are two men who won't compromise. You're too damn stubborn, and everything has to always be your way. And it can make life hard for a woman. It's either accept it or go away."

"Hey, we don't have to make their fight our fight now. Ahh, I'm gonna go feed that mare. All this lovey-dovey talk is getting to me."

Holly looked at Lauren after Bearman left. "What you just said to Jordy is true, isn't it? There is no compromise in that man, is there?"

"No, Holly, there isn't. I know Ab. But that's what makes him the man he is. What's good about them is also what's bad about them. I mean, how many men do you know who would just use you for what they could get out of you? That would say sure, we'll have this fling for a while. And then they're having another fling at the same time. With men like Ab and Jordy, it's that living by their own rules thing. The problem is, if you're going to be their woman, you've got to live by them too. There is no flexibility in those men. It's worth it for me. It's the life I chose, and I love it. But you have to make that decision for yourself. Ab will be all right either way. He's a strong man. You can't keep him down long."

"It's not Ab I'm worried about."

Holly went outside and found Ab sitting on Bearman's spruce chopping block.

He turned when he heard her. "Weather's clearing off. I think you'll be home in two or three days. I know your folks will be happy."

"Yeah. I know Mom's got to be worried sick. We always talk every day. But she'll be okay. It'll give her something to be happy about when I get back home." Holly walked over and put her arms around Ab.

"Ab, I'm sorry I snapped at your this afternoon," she said. "I know you were just being practical. This has just been such an emotional roller coaster for me. You too, I guess, with me just dropping out of the sky on you, literally."

"It's O.K., Holly. It's just circumstances. The way we were thrown together. I guess I let it get a little out of hand. We'll both be fine in a few months. It's not the end of the world."

"Where do you think Rusty is?"

"Nowhere near here, that's for sure."

Chapter 33

THE POWER

Rusty could see activity at the cabin now. The light from the clearing evening sky helped. He had worked his way closer, little by little, studying it all. Making decisions, trying to figure out who was there and how many there were. When he spotted the four wheeler, he felt better. It might not be them. It might be a different quad, but he didn't care. He just had to plan the correct move. Figure out the best way to kill whoever was there. He belly crawled down the trail in the mud with only the rifle. He got off the trail when he felt the breeze shift. He had to stay downwind of the livestock and any dogs or other animals that would give him away.

He wanted them all together, after supper, in the same room. He could storm it then. The AR probably would have been better for this, but he would make do with the bolt gun. He would have surprise on his side. He still knew how to throw a bolt fast. He worked his way through the weeds to a small stand of spruce, just thirty yards from the front door. The cabin had more rooms, and that might be a problem, but he would deal with it. He had been in these situations before.

Patience would win the day. Maybe his luck had changed. If they're here, the man and the woman, it's possible, maybe even probable, that the story's not out. He would simply kill them all. It would die with them. He could take his time, hide the bodies, and take the quad. It would give him the buffer time he needed. He could be out of the country before anyone figured it all out, if they ever did.

A man came out the front door, followed by another man. They were both lean, long-haired men, and they were talking about a plane coming. He heard the taller man say it would be at least two days. That was it, he would have the time he needed. Then the tall man went inside and the woman came out. It was the two of them. Standing there, so easy to kill, targets of opportunity. But he had to wait. The big man had gone out back and was out of sight. Rusty wanted them now, but he would wait. Stick with the plan. He needed them all together in the same room. Then he would execute the plan: to execute them summarily. But Rusty almost gave in to the temptation. He put the reticle up on the man's chest and snicked the safety forward. He took two pounds of slack out of the three-pound trigger. It would be so easy. Just blow his heart out of his chest, throw the bolt, and hit the woman too. But Rusty was a good soldier. He would wait, follow the plan. Then he heard the woman ask the mountain man about him, and the man said Rusty was nowhere near here. Surprise would definitely be on his side.

* * *

Ab and Holly came back in the cabin together, and Lauren could tell that the tension was relieved. Maybe what she had said to Holly helped. Or maybe the two of them had talked and come to an understanding. "Let me get you two a drink."

"I'll get them, Lauren. Keep your seat. I loved that buffalo, by the way," said Ab.

"You should, Ab, you killed it."

Bearman came back in from the corral. He looked at Ab with the bottle in his hand. "Steals booze off of airplanes or anywhere else he can get it."

Ab handed them all a drink. "What can I say. This engine runs on high octane. I gotta get it from wherever I can."

"Always pilferin'."

Lauren felt better about the mood. Holly seemed more relaxed, though not as at ease as she would have liked. Jordy and Ab were back at it, which lowered the tension as well. Then Lauren remembered the necklace she had put on Holly's bed. It was a bead necklace, made by a Tetlin Indian woman in Northway. Lauren wanted Holly to have something from her and Jordy, a memento, to remember her stay here.

"Holly, I left something on your bed that Jordy and I want you to have. I don't think you'll find anything like it in Beverly Hills. It's not much, but it's to let you know how much we have enjoyed having you here."

Holly was surprised. "Well, thank you, I'll go get it."

Holly saw the necklace lying across the pillow and thought it was beautiful. It had small stones of all colors in it. She had seen stones like them, only larger, at the hot spring where she and Ab had camped. She turned to the mirror by the bed to put it on. The bruises on her face were almost gone now, and she thought about how Ab had gotten them all back, all but Rusty.

She heard the door crash open and dropped the necklace to the floor. There was no mistaking the voice.

"Move and die, motherfuckers. You ain't the only one who can move through this country, cocksucker."

Holly could see Jordy in his chair and the look on his face. But he didn't dare move. She took a step closer to the bedroom door and could see Ab sitting on the sofa, and she could make out the end of the gun barrel, one foot from his chest.

"You think you're a slick little cunt, don't you, sticking your fucking nose where it don't belong. Where's your little movie queen?"

"She's gone. Not here."

"You're a lying fuck. She's here somewhere."

Holly saw the gun on the nightstand. Ab's gun. She knew it was cocked and locked. It was always that way. All she could remember was thumb on the safety. She had to keep her thumb on the safety. Just do it like Ab. Just do it like Ab.

Holly never heard the gun go off. She saw the front sight on Rusty's chest as she leaned out, saw the rifle flip out of his hand and blood splatter from his left shoulder. And she shot again and again and again, driving him to the floor.

Rusty couldn't react to the sound other than to cut his eyes to the left. He tried to pull the trigger, but his left arm had already dropped the front of the rifle and it had pulled away from his right hand. He could see the muzzle flashes now, in slow motion, but could not hear the other gunshots. It was the heat in his chest that he felt now, streaks of it. His knees slowly gave out and he sank to the floor unable to will his body to move. He had his eyes and his brain, and he knew they would go fast.

It was good, he thought, the pain went away and he felt right with it. He did his duty for his family, for his country, and finally for himself. He could see her now standing over him holding the .45. Rusty thought of his little boy as he looked into the woman's face and tried to smile.

Her hands were shaking now, the gun still pointed at the man crumpled on the floor. And then she felt Ab's hand on hers, taking the .45 from her.

"You got him, Holly. You did it. You had the power. I told you that you did."

* * *

Ab and Bearman wrapped Rusty in tarps and drug him out to the meat shed. Holly's first shot had been slightly off, hitting Rusty in the upper left arm, breaking the entire left shoulder and causing him to drop the rifle. It had saved Ab's life, and probably the Bearmans' as well. The other three shots had angled through the chest, shredding the man's lungs. It was Ab's first real chance to study his opponent. Holly's first shot had pierced the parachute over an "airborne all the way" tattoo. Ab looked into the man's eyes. The face had special forces written all over it. The arms and legs were muscular, but the stomach had grown a little soft. Still, the man looked like an incarnation of a well-oiled killing machine.

"He'll keep til the plane gets here," Bearman said. "Pretty tough looking hombre. I take that back. He was obviously one tough mother. That would be a damn tough hike for you or me, Wildman."

"No shit. The guy had some willpower. Pretty pissed off at me too," said Ab.

"Well, Wildman, it's over now. He picked the wrong glacier to land on and the wrong boy to pick on."

"Nope, he picked the wrong girl to pick on."

"Damn straight, Wildman. I'm glad you showed her how to pull a trigger today. You think killing this guy will mess with her head?"

"I don't think so. Not for long, anyway. I'll talk with her about it."

"Uh oh, chopsticks and China, here we come," said Bearman.

"No, I just want her to feel what she really feels. Not to feel the way she's been programmed to feel."

Holly was in bed when Ab came back in. He crawled under the covers and held her for several minutes before saying anything.

"I sure am glad I can still put my arms around you."

"What, Ab? Oh, yeah, I am too."

"So what are you feeling, Holly?"

"I don't know, Ab. I just feel blank. But almost satisfied. I mean, after my nerves calmed down, I almost felt good for a few minutes. Then I thought, 'This is wrong. I should feel horrible.' But I don't. I don't feel good now, but I don't feel bad either. But it's definitely different when you're the one pulling the trigger."

"Just feel what you feel, Holly. Don't even consider all the bullshit you've heard about going to pieces after you kill someone. You saved everyone's life in this house. Be proud of that. You don't have to be proud of killing a man, but you have nothing to feel bad about. You're just an old momma bear that protected her cubs, and you should just go on about your business just like she would."

"Animals don't feel guilt, do they?" she asked.

"They don't do anything to feel guilty about. And neither have you, Holly. In fact, I can't imagine you ever having done anything to feel guilty about. I know you've brought me to a place where I've never been. You're like a gift I've been given. Just a constant flow of higher energy that goes into me. And it doesn't take words or consciousness to happen. It just is. The only thing that can mess it up is to think about it. To worry and fret over tomorrow or next week. And it's the same with you right now. Everything that happened this past week, right up to Rusty in that den, wasn't created by you or me. We didn't impose our will on anyone. We reacted without thought. And it's why we're still here. If we just lay here and consciously rehash it long enough, we can talk ourselves into feeling guilty about a lot of things. In my mind, Holly, you and I are beyond reproach on any issue we've encountered." Ab had his arms around Holly with both hands holding hers.

"The world can be so different than I ever imagined it, Ab. So much violence and turmoil thrown on you, and so fast and unexpectedly."

"We almost need it to keep us humble, Holly. The people who get so smug and self-righteous about their positions in life are the ones who never face violence or struggle. They see it on TV, but it doesn't affect them.

So they come up with simple, childish solutions about how to make the world a peaceful place. The only reason people try to hurt us and kill us, Holly, is because they can. The only way to stop violent force is with the same thing in return. It's the only reason I'm still talking to you right now. You responded to it the only way you could. There's nothing else to be said about it, and there's nothing else to think about it."

"I don't know, Ab. I mean, I hear what you're saying and it all sounds good. But the feeling is different. There's a blankness in me. I can't make myself have a feeling about it at all. And that makes me think I might be learning something about myself that I'm not so sure I like. The capability for violence."

"It's the capability to survive, Holly."

"It's not a very pretty way to survive, Ab."

"Get out of denial, kid. You've seen enough this week to understand that concept."

"I guess I am out of denial now. So what do you do after that?"

"You live with it, Holly. You live with it." He pressed his lips into Holly's hair.

Chapter 34

A GLASS HOUSE

Holly lay on her side, six inches from Ab, watching him sleep. The moonlight through the window, accented by the snow, gave a haloed view of the man. It was one version of the man. There were others. She had seen the variations during the past week. But pulling them all together and into the essential man would take more than a week, especially a week like the one they had just been through. Her life, now, felt like chaos in the center of confusion. She had made rotten choices in the past, even during periods of clarity. The entire last week of her life was anything but clear. What kind of a commitment do you make to that, she wondered. She stroked Ab's hair, watching him sleep. It was the same every night. He might as well be in a crib with the other babies. Because that's what it was--childlike, uninhibited sleep. No dreams, no runaway random thoughts were cruising that brain at night. The chest went in, the chest went out. He took deep breaths through the nose, but did not snore.

What did she really know about him, she wondered. A man who would climb a glacier and save your life. He didn't have to do that. He certainly didn't need to. Someone who, without knowing you, would take on your problems and ask for nothing in return. And a man who could kill, on a second's notice, then sleep like this.

Just get on that plane, Holly, she thought. Ab said it in the bush. Learn from it, don't dwell on it. Keep the good stuff. Surviving was good. Life was good. Her life. The one back home with all its southern California complications. Holly tried to catalogue her future life, the real one with movies and scripts and shallow people. At least they were shallow people who didn't shoot at her. But she was only tallying pros and cons.

Holly kept staring at Ab, and then it hit her, the lesson she had learned. It's not what you know that makes you who you are; it's understanding what you don't know. Lying in bed, watching Ab sleep, Holly understood that there were things she did not know, and could not know. And now she knew where it all ended. It ended with the heart.

Holly crawled over onto Ab, waking him. She pushed his long hair back and held his face. "I love you.

I do not know you. I do not know who you are, but I love you."

Ab put his lips against Holly and breathed deeply. "That door's not locked, Holly. And I'll let you in on a secret. My house is glass. And you've already seen in all the rooms. Some of them you like, and some of them you're not sure about. And I've seen in yours. You know what I think? I think it's a pretty place. A little cluttered in some rooms, but a nice place to live and be. And I'm glad I got to see inside." They held each other a while in the moonlight, both breathing softly, and then they fell asleep together.

EPILOGUE

Holly was standing in the police station in Northway. She finished her interview with the police, then made several phone calls back home. She would take a small plane to Tok, another to Anchorage, then jet service to L.A. She would be home by midnight.

Holly walked out of the small inner office into the tiny lobby of the police station. The receptionist sat behind a counter with a small transistor radio playing. A large frame window looked out across the gravel parking lot. The Wrangell Mountains were in the distance to the south. And there was Ab, leaning against his truck, waiting to take her to the airstrip. Then he would drive away, down the Alaska Highway, on to Alabama, and out of her life.

"Just one more paper for you to sign and you can go, Miss Allen," the receptionist said. "You're the most famous person to ever set foot in here."

"Thank you," Holly said. She could hear "Midnight Train to Georgia" playing on the small radio sitting on the woman's desk.

Holly looked out the window at Ab, his long brown hair blowing in the September breeze, a look of acceptance and resignation on his face.

She walked out into the sunshine.

"Did you get your folks?" Ab asked.

"Yeah, they're really relieved."

"Well, you can relax now. You'll be home in just a little while. Then I can watch you in the movies. We better get you to the airstrip. They got your plane ready to go."

Holly put her arms around Ab. "I'm not getting on a plane, Ab."

"Wait a minute, Holly. Now we've talked about this. California and Alabama, and all that stuff in between. Hard to mesh all those things. So much distance. I mean, I know what I want. But then, I don't want things to turn out bad for us. Either one of us."

"It won't, Ab. It can't. The other night you said you wanted me to find the house of truth. Well, Ab, I don't know about that. I don't know if I understand all that. But I do know this. I found the house of love, and it's where I want to live. So we'll just take it one day at a time. One day. Somebody told me that one time. Love can't have a bad day."

"Holly, do you have any idea what you are doing?"

Holly looked up into the big Wrangell Mountains. "I don't have a clue, Ab."

"Well now we're getting somewhere. Come on."

* * *

Ab cranked the truck and the Nickelback CD blasted to life. He turned the volume down. "Sorry about that."

"Am I gonna have to listen to that head banging music all the way to Alabama?"

Ab handed Holly the CD case. "Lord, help me."

Printed in the United States
78159LV00001B